The Oasis of Filth

My Chronicle of the RL2013 Outbreak

A Novel

Part One

Keith Soares

Bufflegoat Books

Original publication date July 4, 2013

Special thanks to my wife, Layla, for giving me the time and feedback to actually do this. Additional thanks to Jeff Yeatman for his copious notes on expanding this world, and to Susan Gd. G. Clutter for pointing out a rather indigestible error.

Edited by Christopher Durso.

Also from Keith Soares

The Oasis of Filth

Part 1: The Oasis of Filth

Part 2: The Hopeless Pastures

Part 3: From Blood Reborn

The Fingers of the Colossus *(Ten Short Stories)*
[Forthcoming]

1

"Noah, you have leprosy," I said to the poor kid as he sat there, nervously sweating despite the coolness of the day. Noah Parker, just 14 years old. I wish I could have saved that poor kid. But more than that, I wish I had understood what I was looking at. He was the first one I ever saw. But obviously not the last.

Some people say, "How could you be so blind?" I tell them the truth. We weren't blind. We saw everything. We just didn't *understand.*

You know, as obvious as something might be, if you've never seen it before — never contemplated the possibility that something universally believed to be fiction might actually be true — then how can you possibly be prepared to accept it, even if it's sitting in your own office, chewing gum, wearing a green and white Wildcats high school football jersey? Or at least that's what I tell myself. After all this time, when you've seen the things that I have, if you don't tell yourself something to keep going, you'll just give up. I'm not quite ready for all that.

Not that I have much choice. Time is not on my side. Noah Parker got the bad news in my office almost 11 years ago. At the time, I was a 52-year-old family practice doctor in central Maryland. I made a good living, and most of the community looked up to me — the guy who made them feel better. Things change. Noah died 18 days later. It's amazing what the mind can recall and what it can forget. Whatever tragedies I went through yesterday — and I'm sure there were some — are all but forgotten in the blur of repetition and the daily effort to keep moving on. But this I remember clearly: In the fall of 2013, Noah Parker walked into my office with a few skin lesions. He told me it started as one, and he ignored it — he couldn't remember, but he thought it might have been from cutting himself while mowing the lawn. That specific lesion was tiny but looked ragged, like it had been torn or bitten. When the third lesion appeared, he was worried. He told his parents once he had six, and came to see me the next day.

I missed the forest, but I saw the trees. Leprosy. Before I went to medical school, I wanted to just go *somewhere* — get away. I knew the next several years of my life would be devoted to the singular cause of graduating and working toward my own practice. So before all that, I traveled to India for escape. My parents told me to be careful, watch out for this or that. For several years already, I'd been a solo backpacker, staying in tiny, rundown hostels every place I had visited, so I assured them that I could do it there, too. In India, with the seed of a medical education about to grow in my mind, I was confronted first hand with leprosy. Aimlessly backpacking, I stumbled across a leper colony, and curiosity took over. I talked to the one doctor I could find there. His English was excellent. He told me how they tickled the faces of young children to detect where they could no longer feel. He showed me what the skin lesions looked like. He told me the cycle of treatment; the isolation he said was required. I ended up looking into leprosy briefly during my freshman year. I learned, most importantly, that it had been cured. Nonetheless, some places like India kept alive the culture of the leper colony. I dug into it pretty deeply for a time. But like most random things, after a while the interest waned.

Then, here was this kid in my office. And it clicked: This looks *familiar*. I dug up information as fast as I could. But in the end, it was just instinct and experience. I know most doctors in the United States, even more experienced ones, would have totally missed it. But I knew: leprosy. When I told Noah, his eyes almost bugged out of his head. His parents were aghast. They blurted the obligatory comments. Was I *sure*? How was this *possible*? I told them that I could be wrong, but I'd seen it before, up close. And I told them that leprosy was completely curable. To me, the physician, that felt like a weight lifted off my shoulders; I could actually *do* something for this kid. Then I looked at his parents. They were shell-shocked. I might as well have told them their son was dying within the hour. The idea that their own flesh and blood had something so horrific as leprosy stunned them beyond words. Noah's mother, who looked like she was clinging to her youth with every fiber, wearing tight jeans and a fashionable yellow top, seemed to age 15 years as she crumbled into her husband's arms. Noah's father, for that matter, had lost his normal ruddy complexion and jovial nature. His eyes glassed over, shining empty above his dark navy sport jacket and white shirt worn with no tie. I stared. Could I be wrong? Did I just send an entire family into a downward spiral on a whim? No, I got it right, I thought to myself. Noah had leprosy.

In the end, it didn't really matter. Because what I missed were the other things. The flu-like symptoms, the anxiety. I was so proud of myself for being able to recognize leprosy that I completely missed it. The kid also had rabies.

2

Leprosy and rabies in one kid. What an unlucky bastard, right? Well, of course, you must be familiar with the story. But maybe you don't know the details. It wasn't just Noah. It was happening in lots of places, all over the world in fact. Again, were we blind? No. Nothing we believed prepared us for something to swoop in so quickly from so many places. It was like a coordinated attack, but there was no general, no army, no battlefield. Every soldier in this attack operated independently. The only cohesion came from the fact that it all happened at the same time. I was focused on the case of Noah, who was getting rapidly worse, with other symptoms I didn't understand. It wasn't until five days later, when Noah lashed out, that I realized my hubris had made me miss the signs.

That fifth day, Noah bit my nurse, Terry Rawlins, on the arm. Tore skin off in his madness. What the hell would make him do that? That's when I realized this wasn't just leprosy. After I'd sedated Noah, had him transferred to a hospital for round-the-clock care, and was done patching up Terry, I started to analyze the other symptoms I was seeing. But give me no credit. That night, I turned on the news just to take a mental break. And there I saw it. Doctors in Georgia had identified three cases of people with leprosy *and* rabies, and were reporting that somehow these conditions had become *intertwined* within the patients — like they happened together. It was such a medical mystery that it appeared at the end of the newscast — not a top story of concern, but an afterthought, to make the audience scratch their heads and have something bizarre to talk about over dinner.

I sat upright in my chair. That explained the other symptoms! Noah definitely had rabies, too. I dialed into the office and looked up his records, then called his parents. After the briefest of pleasantries, I asked, "Was Noah bitten by an animal recently, like a raccoon? Has he been to Georgia recently?" But the answer to both questions was no. Regardless, I told the parents how I believed Noah's other symptoms may stem from rabies. They were incredulous. How could their son — their *own* son, living in America in the 21st century — have both leprosy *and* rabies? They must have thought I was a complete quack. But there was no time for that, rabies doesn't wait. I called the hospital and spoke to Noah's attending physician. He was skeptical. Even after I told him of the cases in Georgia, he found it hard to believe that there was any relation or truth to it.

It wasn't until the next morning that the attending physician started to believe. Noah — fitful from a night of almost no sleep — tore into a rage and tried to break free of his straps, simply from the sight of an orderly bringing in water. Treatment was ordered. It was too late. Terry Rawlins went mad, too. She lasted seven weeks in restraints, with researchers focused on her 24 hours a day.

Soon after, reports came out of Maine, Arizona, Utah. Then from overseas. Patients were cropping up all over with a combination of leprosy and rabies. Doctors tried — unsuccessfully — to treat one or the other, to remove at least part of the problem. Nothing took. Lesions, fever, increasing anxiety, lack of sensation in nerve endings, flattened nose, thickening skin, dementia, rage. All the classic symptoms of leprosy and rabies, combined. And patients got worse, all of them. Restrained and fed through tubes, they could last a really long time, although many died horribly. Or were killed. Sometimes it was quick, like Noah Parker, but sometimes it went on for many, many months before the end.

They called the disease RL2013, a not-terribly-clever nod to rabies, leprosy, and the year of discovery. We mostly called it *the disease*, or just *it*. We still do. "Stay away from him, he's got *it*," or "That baby has *the disease*." We called the infected by another name. Given the symptoms, the physical changes, the mental changes, the bloodlust. The fact that what they had was contagious as hell. These people — people you may have known, may have loved — became deformed, raging lunatics. They weren't some sort of undead monster, they had no magical powers, and you could kill one as easy as you could kill anybody else. But it spread like wildfire, and God help you if one bit you: There was no cure. So despite our best attempts to rationalize the hell around us, we had to admit it was true.

Zombies walked among us. And they were winning.

3

For more than 10 years, we lived in fear. But the funny thing was, it wasn't really fear of the zombies. It was fear of dirt, and what came with it. The government pulled in the walls of the cities — cities were the only things left with any infrastructure — and inside those walls was where we lived, in giant compounds. Well, we called it *pulling in the walls* as a cultural reference, but in truth they had to make the walls. The society that once was home to the freest, proudest people on Earth remade itself along quasi-feudal lines, with pockets of citizens huddled together, struggling through totalitarian rule. Because it kept them safe.

I made it to Washington, DC, and I got inside the walls. Others did the same in New York, Chicago, Houston, Los Angeles, and elsewhere. Some cities fell apart or were overrun. I heard an estimate that about 30 million Americans lived in the cities, which seemed like a lot — but just doing the math from where we started, that meant more than 300 million people were still outside. Even as contagious as the disease was and how fast it could kill, there must have been a lot of people struggling for their lives in what used to be the United States. As well as a lot of zombies. And a lot of dead. God only knew what the numbers looked like everywhere else in the world.

Inside the walls, everything had to be clean. Only by completely sterilizing our environment could we hope to one day overcome the epidemic. That's what the laws said. People were taken away simply for not keeping themselves and their homes and their streets clean. The government said this is why we still had outbreaks. If everyone could work together, keep every inch of the city free from grime or mildew or fungus, we could avoid additional infections. I understood their frustrations, to some degree — after more than 10 years, you'd think we could have solved this. But my experience as a doctor made me question this policy. I knew that some amount of cleanliness was useful to ward off infection, but I also knew that scrubbing a floor wouldn't save you from your neighbor coughing in your face. But always there were stories of some family, some person, some group home, where cleanliness was ignored, the filth built up, and then another outbreak occurred. The talk-show hosts shook their heads and reported on another self-induced tragedy. If only this family had kept to the law, kept their home clean, they wouldn't have become infected. Just the other night, there was a story about two parents and their young daughter. A neighbor went to check on them after not seeing anyone for about a week. When the neighbor entered the unlocked apartment, she found piles of detritus and blooms of mildew. In seconds, she was attacked by the father in a rabid rage and bitten repeatedly. When the authorities got there, they shot and killed the entire family. The neighbor died that evening.

"God has forsaken us!"

"It's the wrath of God, punishing our sins!"

"There is no God!"

"It is the End of Days!"

A lot of people had a lot of ideas about why it all happened. And a lot of those ideas involved God. I didn't know, and wasn't sure how much it mattered. Was there a God, and was that God allowing this to happen? Or maybe God was asleep at the wheel. Maybe it was a test. Or maybe mankind wasn't God's favorite after all.

On the odd occasion that I would tell my story, it didn't help. Many people who heard it compared my Noah — Noah Parker — to the Biblical Noah. But where that Noah rescued all creatures great and small from the flood, Noah Parker, people would tell me, started a flood to drown us all. It didn't matter to the zealots that Noah Parker wasn't the only case. This thing, this disease, appeared all at once in many places. Maybe that actually was a sign of divine intervention. Did the first single-cell organisms manifest in one and only one place? Or did they appear on Earth at a certain time, all over the globe, when the time was right? Could it be that the process of creating new life or new disease was simply following a schedule?

Everything was smaller, more compact. To allow a city to hold more people than it was ever intended for, everyone had to give something up. Houses and apartments were subdivided, methodically, mercilessly, to the smallest possible space that a person or family needed to live. At the same time, almost every sort of personal possession was taken away, so the boxes we lived in weren't just small but spartan. Families were given larger spaces to fit their size, but a single guy like me? I could cook on my stove and flush my toilet all while lying in my bed.

Clothes became a lot simpler. That was something I didn't mind too much. The whole idea of designer clothing became obsolete. There was some variation, but for the most part the government wasn't interested in a fashion show. They ran factories that produced workable, simple clothing. Solid colors, synthetic fabrics. Most people had four or five sets for warm weather, another four or five for cold. We cleaned them all the time, both so that we wouldn't run out and to maintain cleanliness. Even the idea of dressing up disappeared; there were no more suits, ties, ball gowns. In a way, with our flat-colored, synthetic clothing, we looked like we'd stepped out of a silly science-fiction movie, or that we were all on our way to the gym.

All our cell phones were confiscated at the very start. But there were communications between the cities, we knew that. The old wired and wireless methods still seemed to work, although only the government was allowed to use them. I assumed this meant that there were people who worked outside the walls, maintaining the connections and the infrastructure, but I never saw them myself or met anyone who did it. All the news we got came from the government, and that was very little. We had TV and radio, one channel each. The radio station played a lot of classical music, with occasional weather updates. TV wasn't much better. In between news reports on the latest zombie extermination — really thinly veiled threats about keeping clean — they played old movies and shows, mostly black and white, repeated often. It was bizarre to see dapper men in suits and ladies in fancy dresses, jet-setting around a world that no longer existed, or dancing in bright, hugely choreographed routines that parodied our gray, regimented lives. I guess they figured we needed some sort of entertainment. It was so alien, this stylized murk of black and white, that it could have been imported from another planet. Broadcasts would end each night at 11 p.m. with a reminder of the basic rules of cleanliness and stern statements about following government laws.

We always tried to stick to ourselves, stick to small groups. It was a lot safer. The more people you interacted with, the more likely one of them would end up infected. Even the hint of a rumor about infection brought the authorities in droves. Many people felt that turning in their neighbors might convey some extra benefit to them or their family. Backstabbing was commonplace. As for the government, its officers were covered head to toe in pristine white hazmat suits, and swooped in like anonymous destroyers, took what they wanted — who they wanted — and left without a word, without a trace. And always they found evidence of some lack of cleanliness to point to as the culprit. How could they not? Who could keep every speck of their lives spotless at all times?

So that was why we lived in fear. Life is naturally messy. But we did all we could to get rid of the mess. Any sudden discovery of mold in a dark corner was enough to give a person heart palpitations as they rushed to scrub every nook before word got out. In fear — fear of the zombies, fear of the dirt, fear of the government, fear of each other — people would do a lot of crazy things. A neighbor might turn you in if he noticed something he deemed unusual, like you wringing out a mop more than a few times. And sometimes, people would turn you in just because they didn't like you or they wanted something you had. When the government came to get you, there was no reasoning with them, no argument. You just went away.

In fear, we followed the rules. We tried to stay small. We took no risks.

"Stay clean. Stay alive." It was our mantra.

4

Given how small my social circle became, it's a wonder that I ever met anyone new at all. Prior to the outbreak, I spent my days as a happy and probably smug bachelor. I think my position of relative power as doctor in a small town gave me too much self-importance. Now that all that was gone, I would sometimes think about how many chances I'd had to make a life with someone else, maybe even gotten married. I was into my sixties, and knew that possibility was dead. I spent a lot of time with my own thoughts, which can make a person unfit for social interactions. Some of my younger neighbors thought of me as a grumpy old man. Then I met Rosalinda. It was random, like many things. As much as we tried to keep to ourselves, there were still the necessities of living. Most notably, you had to get your food somewhere. The city regulated all food production and kept registered production facilities along its borders. Were we eating fresh-grown food or something out of a laboratory? I suspected a combination. But we lived with it. I got mine from the Capitol Hill Community Food Dispersal Center, more commonly called the FDC.

The FDC was housed in the large, red-brick buildings that once made up Eastern Market, a popular indoor and outdoor marketplace where people would go to buy a range of fresh foods and other goods before the disease. Now we just lined up for our ration boxes. The Eastern Market buildings worked well for this purpose, because they were big and the government could contain people long enough to push them through the line efficiently.

The woman I would come to know as Rosalinda was a strange sight, rather young, pretty, perhaps a dozen people ahead of me in line. She wore a basic white synthetic t-shirt and matching skirt. In another time, she might have looked like she was dressed for a round of tennis at the country club. Here, her basic outfit was mirrored by several other women. Clothing options were fairly limited, but somehow she stood out. Having done the dance of the government ration line with the same neighbors for nearly 10 years, a new face was incredibly unexpected. Although rare, we still had cases of RL2013 inside the city, and they always involved elements of mystery, like new faces or unknown places. I have to admit, my first thoughts were fear and distrust, but they were mixed with a strange interest. How on Earth did someone new get here, and *why*? Did we need to be careful around her? Movement around the city was controlled. The government assigned jobs, housing, places to get food. But beyond that there was the self-imposed, self-regulating control of the people. No one wanted anything new, *anyone* new, because that was change, and change felt dangerous. We were a tremendously paranoid society. I noticed other eyes watching her. She was an outsider. She could be infected. Even 10 years after the outbreak, the disease spread. It was slower now, but it happened. And here she was, where we got our food. What was she doing taking it from us? If the government transferred her here, it said something about their stranglehold on information that they wouldn't even tell us why.

My rational mind tried to turn the tide. There could be any number of good reasons why she was here. It didn't happen often, but people did relocate. We all still had to do our jobs, to keep the small wheels of our confined society spinning and to earn a living. Producing food, making and distributing medicine, policing for outbreaks, maintaining the walls, keeping up the government's elaborate bureaucracy — it was all necessary. If for nothing else than to keep the people's minds off things like revolt. But sometimes those jobs disappeared.

As I shuffled along in line and got my ration box, I considered these options, but generally tried to retreat into myself, the way we all did so well. Then I heard the muffled sounds of trouble. Looking toward the commotion, I saw the strange young woman surrounded by several angry-looking men. They had their hands on her ration box and were saying something she didn't like. She hissed back that she just wanted to be left alone, trying to stay as quiet as possible. I could tell this was going to get very bad very quickly. I looked toward the government guards, clad in their pristine navy-blue uniforms, holding their shiny black firearms. *No one* ever wanted to attract the guards' interest. It wasn't good for your long-term health.

Immediately, I rushed over, cutting between the woman and one of the men. "What's the problem here?" I said.

"Keep out of it, or you'll regret it," one man said — a guy I had seen in the FDC probably once a month for many years. He was maybe 15 years my junior, stronger and taller, with a pointed nose and a close-cropped haircut. He squinted at me, recognizing me, but now distrusting my sudden interest in what he was doing.

"They're trying to take my ration," the woman interjected.

"Be quiet," another of the men said, this one a decade or more younger than me, with the same bullethead look as his partner. He closed ranks so that his black-shirted torso blocked some of the guards' view. I noticed he had a number of homemade tattoos. That told me a lot. A needle could be a very dangerous, dirty thing. There were no formal tattoo parlors anymore, but certain types of people kept up the practice in secret. It was a private little rebellion that made their usually very small minds feel superior. I had to be careful around these two.

But even 10 years into this new world, I guess I retained some sense of right and wrong. Some need for justice and propriety. "She's with me," I said.

"What're you talking about?" the first man scoffed. "She's never been in here with you before."

"I'm telling you, she's with me. Cousin of mine. Lost her job across town and got transferred. She's staying in my uncle's old apartment." In the back of my mind, I was amazed at how easy the lies came.

"Like hell," he frowned, making another tug at her rations. Behind him, I saw one of the guards tilting his head, looking in our direction. I leaned in to talk quietly.

"Listen. In about 30 seconds, that guard is going to decide he doesn't like the look of this, and all of us are going to end up nothing more than a bad memory. Either you let go of the box and she and I walk out without trouble, or I make sure we all go down together."

He leaned back, eyes widening. "Are you threatening me?" He was taken aback by my boldness. He balled his hands into fists. It looked like a common practice for him. That was another sure sign that he wasn't bright: The infected were violent. Most sane people avoided any semblance of violence, for fear of a one-way ticket to government confinement.

"You've got about 20 seconds to decide," I said. The guard was definitely staring in our direction. The man started to turn around to see if I was telling the truth. "Ah, ah — you turn around and he'll *know* we don't want him over here. That'll be the end."

He paused. His fingers loosened as the tiny wheels in his mind spun. "Fine. But get the hell out of here. Now." He shoved the box back into the young woman's hands and faded into the crowd coming out of the building. Out of the corner of my eye, I noticed the guard had turned his head away — someone else had done something that distracted him.

"Let's go, before this gets worse." The young woman just nodded and followed me.

* * *

"My name is Rosalinda," she said as we walked hurriedly away from the building. I grunted a response. She continued walking beside me, then after a pause said, "Thank you."

Rounding a corner and putting the FDC out of view, I turned to her. "What are you really doing here?"

"Huh?" She was surprised at the blunt question. "I... uh..."

I stopped. "Who are you? Why are you here? The trouble doesn't end just because I helped you out back there. People don't like strangers."

"Don't you think I know that?" she said. "Don't you think I feel the same? I *had* to come here. It's my mom."

"What about your mom? Is she someone from the neighborhood? What's her name?"

"Sonya Menendez. 12th and D."

"Don't know the name," I said. "What does she look like?"

"You wouldn't have seen her for a long time. She's been housebound, barely surviving on handouts from a couple of kind neighbors. But now she's dying."

I stepped back without thinking. "Oh *shit.*" What had I gotten myself into?

"It's not that!" Rosalinda looked panicked, and angry, too. "She doesn't have the disease. She's just old. I lived in Northwest ever since the walls closed. Seemed close enough to mom so that we could both live our own lives. I didn't know how bad off she was until a friend at work passed along the message from a coworker who lives here on the Hill. So I had to come. To help her. I applied for transfer and my office accepted. I do medical research."

I knew there was a small lab in the area, but I was skeptical. Rosalinda pleaded silently at me with her eyes. I looked her up and down, trying to assess her trustworthiness. That's when I noticed her bracelet. Little tiny bits of colored fabric woven together, red, yellow, blue, green. Just wisps. I assumed she did it by hand. I tried to think if other people wore similar things, and came up with nothing. It was simple, but unique. It made me think she was somehow more... *human*.

She saw me staring at it and cocked her head to the side, as she moved her arm and tried to shield the bracelet from my view. She seemed embarrassed that I'd noticed it. I'm sure she was trying to get a read on me, too.

"I'm here in this neighborhood now," she said. "And I really could use an actual friend, so the neighbors don't start thinking I'm some crazy loner, here to take all their food and infect them."

I looked at her. And she smirked. So that's how I, at the ripe age of 63, became friends with a beautiful 32-year-old woman. But it was really her mind I most admired.

5

The Garden of Eden. Paradise. Utopia. Shangri-La. Ours was called "The Oasis."

Somewhere out beyond the city walls, The Oasis was a place where people were said to live freely, without fear of government, infection, dirt, attack. A community from the time before, where none of today's worries penetrated inside. Heaven.

In other words, a fantasy.

There were plenty of rumors about The Oasis, but of course, not one of the people talking about it had been outside the walls in 10 years. In office break rooms or playing chess in the park, they would say with utter certainty, "It's in Mexico." "No, Brazil." "No, it's in Kansas." I ignored the nonsense.

Rosalinda — who I had come to call just "Rosa" — and I spent a lot of time together, at least after work. There were too many doctors in DC for me to have continued my practice, according to the government hack that decided such things, so I was shifted to a large government pharmacy, filling prescriptions. It kept me alive, so I guess I didn't mind too much.

But Rosa was kind of important. She worked as a microbiologist with the National Institutes of Health, in a small lab they'd set up in Southeast. She was working with the government to find a cure. Once the initial wave of paranoia swept past, she made a few friends in the neighborhood. People constantly asked her what she knew — were we close? Any luck today? But in reality, she was told very little about the big picture, and just tasked to focus on the bacteria *Mycobacterium leprae* and *Mycobacterium lepromatosis*, which cause leprosy. She would tell me of minor triumphs, sometimes major failures, and the doldrums of working day after day on something that seemed to have little purpose or goal, and no discernable outcome.

We had dinner together often, and you might think that a romance was blooming. Maybe it was, but I was twice her age and never truly pushed it. We would talk for hours, and then I would head back to my apartment. With her mom's health in rapid decline, I was also useful to have around, simply to help out with day-to-day chores.

We just liked to talk. Our backgrounds in science and medicine gave us a similar mindset that made conversations feel comfortable. When we weren't discussing The Oasis, we'd wonder about the world outside the walls, or remember the time before the outbreak, or just chat about the latest news. Anything to keep our minds occupied. And sometimes it seemed like we'd keep a conversation going just to spend time together.

We did calculations on the disease outside the cities. Three hundred million left outside, 10 years ago. The disease seemed to be 100-percent infectious if a person was bitten or wounded by a zombie, resulting in a 100-percent mortality rate, eventually, from what we knew. But if you could avoid the zombies, maybe keep your own little space clear of the filth that stirred up the disease in the first place, you'd have a chance, or at least we thought so. Nonetheless, before the outbreak, around 3 million people per year died in the United States. Imaging a landscape without medical treatment, without any guaranteed food, we guessed that number might be much, much higher, maybe 25 million a year. Sure, there were likely births to offset some of that, but even putting the attrition rate at 20 million a year, the U.S. had lost 200 million people. That was our guess. More than half the country, gone. But that still left 100 million potential zombies to carry on the infection. And that wasn't counting the possibility that animals could carry it as well. Looking at the trajectory, we could see the outbreak couldn't last forever. The problem was, neither could the human race.

When the discussion would get overly serious and scary, we'd change the subject to something lighter. Dealing with an ill family member is a grueling affair, so there was comfort in just falling into a chair and talking about *anything else* with someone who understood the value of distraction. I asked about her bracelet. She laughed.

"Yep, I made it. I was just so *bored* of everything looking the same. When something wears out — a shirt, bed sheet, whatever — I like to take a little sliver of it before it goes to the recycling center. I keep it small, so it doesn't attract too much attention. And I make little things, bracelets."

"You have more than one?" I asked, raising my eyebrows.

She didn't reply. Instead, she stood up and walked to a small table, opening a drawer in the front. Inside, I saw dozens of little bracelets, in an array of colors.

* * *

Her mom died of natural causes a little more than five weeks later. There was a small, unassuming ceremony monitored by two bored-looking government agents who failed miserably in their attempt to blend in. This was common practice at funerals in the city — to ensure that the death wasn't related to the outbreak.

Rosa was devastated. Even in our world of hardship and fear, the loss of a parent was the permanent shutting of a door. At the same time, it opened another door to the realization that, after all, we were mortal; we all died.

Everyone says they know this, but losing a parent makes it hit like a hammer blow.

I kept going to Rosa's mother's apartment for dinners and other visits, and in short order just thought of it as Rosa's apartment. Sometimes Rosa would come to my place, since there was no one left at hers who needed attention, but we rarely tempted fate by having her walk home alone at night. Sometimes our conversations would turn to The Oasis.

One night at Rosa's apartment, after a light dinner, as she and I finished meticulously cleaning, drying and storing the dishes, she turned to me. "Wouldn't it be amazing? Just to stop all this. To go back to something normal?" I stopped, lowering the plate I'd been about to place back on its shelf. There was a twinkle in her brown eyes as she looked away, past me. I could see the dream meant something to her. It gave her hope. There was no way I was going to laugh and take that away from her.

After that, the topic came up more frequently. It seemed Rosa was organizing — in her head — a sort of compendium of thoughts about The Oasis. The most important detail she worked to figure out was simple: Where was it? Just answering that one question would be life-altering. For that alone would mean *it really existed*. The details of how people lived there, how many were there, all that would be far less important. Just *where was it?*

When people would say Kansas or Brazil or Mexico, it was clear they were generalizing. Brazil is a rather large place, and it was unlikely that the haven of all humanity set up shop in the deepest rainforest. Without any government backing, it seemed more likely that natural diseases like malaria would have a devastating effect there. That was one aspect of our situation that always amused me; in the midst of the most horrific outbreak in human history, we were still on the hook for such everyday maladies as the common cold, even athlete's foot or gingivitis. But these things were rare in the pristine society of the city — and if you did have anything unusual, you kept it quiet, for fear of disease rumors. Besides, you had to think fate was a twisted, cruel mess if you died from a zombie bite because you couldn't run away fast enough due to the discomfort of athlete's foot.

Because she worked as a government researcher, Rosa would sometimes get "Official Government Communications" — I've added the capitalization because somehow that's how she pronounced it every time. In her research, she had access to several computers, linked together with her colleagues and connected to some sort of repository of data — things the government had collected, other research that was useful as reference. She had extremely controlled access to email. She was allowed to send and receive messages from her colleagues related to work and office interests, but anything social or personal was forbidden. Breaking this rule could result in suspension or even termination. And you didn't want to be unemployed in the current world setting. The Internet seemed long dead, and even if it were still around, random browsing would have been forbidden as well. I imagine Rosa was tempted to search for The Oasis in her data systems, although I'm sure she could guess the outcome would be quite dangerous. In any event, Rosa did get messages from the government, usually in the form of email, but sometimes it required a real human being to deliver it to the lab where she worked. Because she was based on the Hill and not at NIH proper, the messengers often stayed for a while, whether to rest or just simply avoid their superiors for a while. On these occasions, when she could either hear something in their conversation or even ask a direct question without seeming like she was collecting information, Rosa would learn what she could about The Oasis. Actual news that wasn't from the know-nothing people in the neighborhood.

From these infrequent visits, a seed was planted. Rosa began to firmly believe that The Oasis, in some fashion, was real and existed in the western part of South Carolina, along the border with Georgia. Multiple hints and rumors talked about a vast emptiness outside the eastern walls of Atlanta, and a similar emptiness west of Columbia, South Carolina. In that sprawling expanse where someone should have been straggling, surviving, scraping by, the government wasn't seeing anyone. The occasional zombie, yes, but never any *people*. If our estimates were anywhere near correct — and I'm sure the government had much better numbers — there were still those 100 million people who should be around. But no one was ever sighted in that region. The area Rosa focused on had big lakes, some parkland, and plentiful forests. And it was just north of Augusta, a city that had been walled for about three-and-a-half years before falling apart. The government would admit to nothing, but the prevailing rumor was that Augusta fell because of some internal rebellion.

In Rosa's mind, the countryside was perfect, the rebellion in Augusta spoke of a starting point and possible resources for a new community, and the empty swathes told her something was different there. In only a few weeks, she became sure that The Oasis was real, and sat about 500 miles south of us down Interstate 95. Her growing certainty had two simultaneous effects on me: It was intoxicating, making me want to believe, and it terrified me. Had this person I'd come to care about so much lost touch with reality and pinned her hopes on a phantom?

As a man of science, I tried to offer alternate, more rational theories. It was possible that some other disease could have ravaged the area. Or there was radiation or some other contaminant that made it unfit for human habitation. Or maybe the reports were just wrong. Rosa would listen to my counterpoints, but she was headstrong. She'd parry every argument. Why wouldn't any of those other reasons bubble up from her information channels, she wondered, especially with a government that wanted to be in total control and typically left nothing to mystery? Shouldn't she have heard *something*?

There was more to be concerned about. Neighbors and coworkers slowly began to realize that she was plying them for any information. She would laugh it off and say she was just talking nonsense to pass the time, but when it happened repeatedly it was harder not to notice. At least one of the government messengers paused, gave her a long look, and then left her building without saying anything. Was her obsession putting her — perhaps even both of us — in jeopardy? It made me hesitate.

As I said, we spent *most* nights together, but not all. So it was not that unusual if I declined her invitation. I found myself turning her down sometimes for no good reason, although now I'm ashamed to admit that. I think her fascination with a fantasy made my older bones and older mind tired sometimes. And that's why on May 23rd, a date I'll always remember, I wasn't there when they took her.

6

You know how you could tell the government cars on the street from anyone else? Because only the government had cars anymore.

It was a picturesque spring evening, the weather cool but not cold, the bright sun beginning to set, making for long shadows and brilliantly illuminated west-facing walls. I was walking home, and a sense of guilt forced me to pass Rosa's street and pause to look in the direction of her apartment. I spotted a black vehicle just as its doors closed and engine revved, and watched it race northward. Immediately I knew what had happened. I ran to her apartment building as fast as I could and scaled the stairs more quickly than a person my age should. My heart, already pounding, stuttered when I found her front door open, no one inside. I ran to the window and craned my head to see where the car was going. But I knew. Everyone knew where they took you. Just as everyone knew you never came back.

Bolling Air Force Base, on the banks of the Potomac River. It was in Southeast, just over the bridge. They'd go north, turn east on Pennsylvania Avenue, cross the river, and then go south. I didn't hesitate.

Tucked behind her building, Rosa had a bike; it was an old, black, metal contraption. Since no one had cars, bikes with baskets were the preferred alternative when getting supplies. She liked to ride hers to work most days. With no sense in my head, I grabbed it, jumped on, and headed after them. Neighbors ran into the street to gape at me, the lunatic. I'm certain they believed they were seeing me for the last time. Rosa, too. So be it, I thought.

I could never catch up to the car, but knowing they were heading to Bolling was all that mattered. I kept going. I turned east onto Pennsylvania, pedaled as fast as my old ass could. The car was barely visible ahead.

Minutes later the black government sedan swerved left, then right. It went off the road just before the bridge and slammed into an abandoned fast-food joint. I wasn't close enough to see much detail. There were people spilling out. One ran for the river. My God, was that her?

It was. Rosa ran toward the river as shots were fired. One clipped a tree near her head, and my heart leapt into my throat. I stopped the bike. One of the men from the car ran after her, while another spoke into a handheld radio, probably calling for a slew of backup that would soon clog every road and pathway in the area.

But no one knew I was doing anything wrong. Sure, the local civilians gathering around the accident looked at me in that awful way reserved for strangers, but I could just ride home and be done. Go back to my life.

The hell with that. At that point, at that age, Rosa was my life. I would go with her or die trying. I turned the bike down a side street and raced for the river. In two blocks, I spied the government agent who was chasing her. I took the risk and biked up to him.

"You looking for a dark-haired woman?" I panted. "I think I saw her running up 11th."

He looked at me with a sneer of disgust and suspicion. "Why are you helping me?" he asked.

"Hey, I scratch your back, maybe you'll scratch mine," I said.

"You people, always the same," he said. He considered it for a second, then asked, "Where on 11th?" I mentioned a spot a block north. Enough to get him out of the way. The sun dropped behind the horizon as he thought about it.

"You realize what happens to you if you're lying to me." It wasn't a question. I nodded. He pulled out a device and pointed it at me, presumably taking my photograph. Then he walked off toward 11th Street.

I waited for him to get out of view, then jumped back on the bike. I figured I could outrun Rosa if she was just following the river south. I was right. I had to jockey the highway, but I caught up to her on Water Street, just off Maine. She was walking as nonchalantly as she could manage, only occasionally looking over her shoulder. I stopped the bike and she saw me.

"Go home. *Please*," she said, walking even faster.

"You know I'm not going to do that," I said.

"Don't waste the rest of your life on me!"

"The way I see it, you were pretty much the only enjoyable thing in my life this past year, so if you don't mind, I'm just going to stick with you. Where are we going?"

She stopped and looked at me. A combination of incredulousness, relief, love, fear. "I have no idea," she said.

"Okay, then I do. Come on."

7

We headed for the waterfront near the old, abandoned monuments. I had an idea that, while even dumber than racing after Rosa on the bike, might just work. We passed all of the boats docked on the Anacostia River, because while they would do the job, they were big, excessive solutions. But more than that, I had no idea how to start any of them. It was a long walk, but eventually we arrived near the Jefferson Memorial, neglected and forsaken by a country that had turned its back on its highest ideals.

I stared up at the rounded marble hulk, thinking about how far we had come from the days of Thomas Jefferson, author of the Declaration of Independence, founding father of a great country, now a sad, besieged city-state terrified of zombies and mold and its own citizens. If it weren't all so terribly true, it would have been funny. I remembered walking under the dome, many years before the outbreak, and I recalled the words inscribed there: "I have sworn upon the altar of God eternal hostility against every form of tyranny over the mind of man." If true, Jefferson, a founder of our government, would now be that same government's sworn enemy.

I made my way around the Tidal Basin to a tiny dock that once offered boats for tourists — small craft, easy to control, from what I remembered. The tourists were long gone, but a few of the boats still bobbed on the sick, oily water. I stared. Paddleboats. Really? Was this another cruel twist of fate? Couldn't we just escape in a canoe, or something a little more... *respectable*? No, we found only abandoned paddleboats. I was wondering if my so-called plan was turning out to be a joke after all. But we chose one, quite at random, and got aboard. Thankfully, despite 10 years of being ignored, its pitted fiberglass hull stayed afloat, and we started to pedal. But it was *dirty*. It terrified us to touch the thing. There were layers of filth, beyond anything we'd seen in years. I had visions of contracting the disease simply from touching the boat. But we went onward.

My God, the boat was loud! How would we escape the city without being detected? Water slapped with every movement of the pedals. Our hearts sank. We may as well have shouted, "We're escaping!" every 30 seconds to add to the sonic overload.

As it turned out, no one cared. DC had become a walled city to keep zombies out, but it seemed to bother very little with keeping anyone in. I suppose when you could avoid having one or two extra mouths to feed, you were fine with people disappearing. What a model of efficiency. Our government had created a society so organized that it knew that losing a citizen could actually make caring for everyone else easier. How shrewd! But we had yet to realize all of this, so we tried to paddle quietly, slowly, over to Northern Virginia. It must have made a comical scene, the most ridiculous escape in history, although I suppose no one ever saw it. Or if they did, they didn't care.

We reached Arlington in full dark. The only lights were behind us, in DC, since Arlington, Alexandria, and the other surrounding cities had largely been abandoned in the pullback. Stepping off the boat, onto land, with Arlington National Cemetery spreading up the hill to our right, overgrown but still recognizable, we felt like astronauts taking their first steps on another world. I'd been here before, many times. But 10 years of changes... well, it was a lot to take in.

We took one look back at DC.

"What now?" she asked.

"Good question." I scratched my head. "Jesus, there could be zombies anywhere. We can't just sit here all night." So we moved.

I remembered — and, like I said before, it's funny what you remember — that Interstate 395 was right there, just to our left. In the daylight, we could follow that to 95, our path south. But for now, shelter was the only concern. Too nervous and bewildered to go far, we walked straight ahead, to a marina in front of the Pentagon. It was dark and seemingly inactive, but filled us with an unbearable fear of the unknown. We found a boat that was still afloat and thankfully wasn't overrun with untold grime, and we climbed aboard. In minutes we were both asleep, lying above deck, close together in the cool evening air of spring.

* * *

Hours later, with the moon gone and darkness all around, with DC's light shimmering so near and impossibly far away, we awoke to a sound. It was a scraping, a scritch-scratching on the dock. It could have been a raccoon — it *should* have been a raccoon. But I felt it in my bones before I even saw anything. It was a zombie.

We propped ourselves up quietly. It hadn't noticed us yet. I got the feeling that scanning the dock might be part of its nightly routine, but who knew. I'd never sat so close to one of these creatures and just... *studied it*.

If it hadn't been for its rather feral motions, it would have been hard to declare it anything other than a human being. It — she —

was female. Maybe mid-40s, Caucasian. But she could have been in her 20s. Age was hard to tell. She looked ragged. Her clothes were too filthy to clearly recognize, but looked like a button-up shirt, possibly flannel, and jeans, torn and covered with layers of dirt. The skin on her face at this distance appeared... bumpy. Her hair was a tangled mess, and her shoes seemed to be long gone. She breathed with the labored rasp of an upper respiratory infection, and cocked her head to one side. She was agitated but not enraged. Her eyes had a milky appearance and she didn't seem to see very well; she spent a lot of time scavenging with her hands, which were clearly deformed. We watched, terrified and amazed, finally laying eyes on the monster we'd feared for so long.

And she stopped. With an almost casual manner, she turned toward us. Slowly, twitching, she shambled to the foot of the pier where our boat was tied. She took a step out onto the pier, wincing and licking her lips. She stopped, sniffed the air. I stiffened, willed myself not to breathe, felt Rosa next to me do the same. I stole a glance at her; she was frozen with fear. I thought *Please, Rosa, just stay still and be silent.* And my right hand, the one propping me up, slipped. I caught my slide with a dull *thump*, my elbow hitting the deck. The zombie flinched, looking right at us. For a split second, it seemed I got away with it. The zombie looked confused. Then that expression gave way to pure fury, her lips pulling back to expose rotted teeth. As Rosa and I scrambled to get out of the way, she lunged.

Her gnarled foot stepped off the pier, toward the boat. And she missed. Rage filled her face, just inches from us, as she fell into the water with a loud splash, followed by a solid thud — possibly her head hitting the hull of the boat. She splashed with even greater hatred, with increasing wildness. It was like she wasn't trying to get out of the water, but just trying to get all of it *off of her.* Again and again, she fell below the surface, then shot up with loud, liquid gasps and panicked splashing.

We scanned in every direction. Nothing we knew could have prepared us for this, sitting alone, outside the city walls, with a zombie making enough noise to wake the dead. Would the zombie's terrible bleating bring more like her? We stood on the boat, too terrified to get off, too afraid to turn our back on the drowning zombie, and too fascinated by this intense experience to do anything but watch.

It seemed like eternity. The zombie finally gasped, splashed, and sank for the last time. For a long while afterward, we felt like we could see her face underwater, staring up at us with icy hatred. We kept scanning the marina. No other zombies appeared. Maybe there were none close enough to hear. Maybe they simply didn't care, each locked in their own dementia. And yet part of me, the primal fear part, thought they were just waiting until we made a move.

We spent the rest of the night sitting back to back on the deck of the boat. We both dozed off momentarily here or there, but each time we awoke with a start, not only jolting ourselves but scaring the holy hell out the other. We never truly rested again that night. When I did sleep, I dreamed of deformed hands emerging from cold, black water.

8

The next morning, our eyes were glued to the water as we stepped back onto the pier. The Potomac isn't terribly deep, but it's muddy as hell, and the water was usually greenish and murky. I may have seen something down there in the muck. I didn't want to dwell on it. After we passed over the gap, we kept walking to dry land and didn't look back.

We walked down the George Washington Parkway to the ramp for 395 and turned toward the right, away from DC. There was no wall on the south side of the city, facing us, because the river provided enough of a natural defensive barrier. I might have given the city one last look, but I don't recall, and actually would be surprised if I had. Funny, not knowing if I'd ever see it again, and not sparing it a memorable last look, not even up there on the highway, where you could take in the whole city. I guess survival and movement seemed more important at the time. We knew zombies weren't just creatures of the night, so we proceeded quietly and kept looking around. Walking in the middle of a wide highway gave us some solace, because we felt that at least we would see if something approached. There were cars abandoned here and there that blocked our view and made for potential zombie hideouts, but most of them were on the other side of the highway, heading toward the city. Either those poor saps made it in or they didn't, there was no way to know.

We made our way southwest. A short while later, as we walked in the middle of the three empty traffic lanes, we crossed under a pedestrian bridge. Two zombies appeared on the bridge, probably 20 feet above us. The bridge was walled by a chain-link fence they couldn't break through, or so I hoped. The one closest to the fence noticed us first. He looked to be a young black male. As we got closer, I could see he was missing one eye and bleeding from both hands and his face. Our presence enraged him, and he leaped at the fence to get to us, crashing into the woven metal again and again. It was pointless. A pedestrian bridge over a major highway is going to be designed to prevent suicide jumpers as its first priority. Flailing, the zombie bloodied himself even worse. We moved to avoid the splatter, which was disgusting and difficult.

From the other end of the bridge, the second zombie heard the commotion and ran in our direction. He also was male, but bigger, with dark, matted hair and a white t-shirt emblazoned with a day-glo logo I didn't recognize. As the first zombie railed against the fence trying to get to us, the second one launched into him, and they both collapsed to the deck of the bridge. We passed under as they carried on a brutal fight, tearing at each other. In minutes, the larger one had killed the other, standing up with blood now coating his t-shirt, hands, and face. He continued to circle the body, swatting and kicking, making guttural noises, shaking his head. We continued farther down the road and out of sight as quickly as possible.

Along with our experience the night before, the bridge incident made me aware that we needed some sort of weapon for protection. I found a solid dead branch downed on the side of the highway, tested it for weight and comfort, snapped off some errant parts, and began using it as a walking stick. I figured at least I'd have something in my hand if anything rushed at us. Rosa found another stick, a little smaller, for herself.

Around midday, we reached the Capital Beltway. The one-time world-famous border between the U.S. political establishment and everyone else. We passed through the complex cloverleaf — there must've been 12 lanes of pavement — threading around and through several huge pileups of cars. There was a tractor-trailer on its side that looked to have been carved out for shelter, now abandoned. Inside the trailer, we could see a small table with a bowl on it, set for a meal. The view immediately made me recognize how hungry I was. What an oversight. I had no idea what to do. Look for supplies nearby? Try to forage or hunt? Every possibility seemed absurd or dangerous as hell. Not having the first clue what native plants to eat, or how to hunt, we made our way toward some of the large buildings that lined the highway. It took most of the rest of the day to find anything edible, but finally, a couple hours before sundown, we stumbled into a bit of treasure trove.

In a parking garage, a beat-up old Nissan two-door sedan had crashed into one of the support beams. The driver, long dead and unidentifiable, clearly had been torn up by a zombie. On the passenger seat, there was a cardboard case of canned beans, wrapped in plastic. Rosa had the bright idea to pop the trunk. There we found other canned goods, bottled water, and even a can opener. The poor dope's emergency prep kit didn't help him, but we both silently gave him thanks.

We opened two cans of refried beans, each of which had a strange taste but were edible. They were similar to a bean paste we'd get in rations from time to time back in the city. We ended up scarfing down a can and a half each. We found a slightly ripped backpack and several fabric shopping bags, loaded up as much as we could carry, and scouted around the parking garage for a place to sleep. It looked like it would rain, so we ended up sleeping on the landing at the top level of the staircase because it was indoors, was the cleanest place we could find, and had working doors that hopefully would provide at least some barrier. Thankfully, other than the rain, the night was uneventful.

9

"Are you sure?" Rosa asked suddenly, during our second day of walking.

"About...?" I asked.

"This. Me. The Oasis."

I stopped walking, and looked around at the repetitive landscape of 95 South. Border trees and pavement. Cars and trucks huddled in clusters, sometimes abandoned, sometimes crumpled together in a wreck. "Yeah." I didn't need to think about it, but I did anyway. "Yeah, I am. Well, I'm sure about you. The Oasis? We'll see. To be honest, I think you're in for a disappointment, but I hope you're right. Even if there is an Oasis, it's a big world; it might not be where you think.

"But you and I both know we can't go back anymore anyway. You were already marked and grabbed by the government, so you show up and you're done. Me? At this point, I've gone missing from my job, my apartment, my neighborhood. It's enough to cause a lot of suspicion. Even if they didn't take me right away, it wouldn't take long. Besides, as easy as it was to get *out* of the city, I seriously doubt we could get back *in*. You saw that line of cars back there, piled up outside DC. They don't just throw open the doors for anyone who walks up. Particularly people that are wanted by the law in the first place."

She looked away. "You... you gave up your life for me and my crazy ideas, you know?" The weight of knowing this was evident on her face.

I shrugged, grinned. "Eh. I'm 63, I live alone in a walled city full of paranoid people, and I'm a pharmacist for the government. Mostly I just count little colored pills all day long. This is actually an improvement." She laughed. I don't think we ever talked about it again. It was settled.

"But I do need to ask." I gave her a sidelong glance. "How'd you crash that car?"

She stopped and smirked. The same smirk I saw outside the FDC that first day. "Men, even men who wield the power of the government, still don't understand women. We can just do crazy things, and you all... *believe it*." She laughed. "I screamed that the handcuffs were burning my skin and they bought it. And I suppose their ego told them I was too small to cause trouble. But once the handcuffs were off, I just had to reach out and pull the wheel. That's it."

I chuckled. "Smart cookie," I said, admiringly. "You could've died in the crash, you know?"

"Wasn't I dead already?"

10

We walked all day. It was warm, and carrying our supplies made it a lot harder. We continued south, trudging along the wide swath of pavement formerly known as Interstate 95. I guessed the width of the road to be about 25 feet, three lanes for cars, shoulders on both sides, but still our forward progress could be slow. In addition to the abandoned or wrecked cars in various stages of decomposition, the road itself could be trouble; cracks, divots, and potholes made us careful with our steps, and in places where there were bridges, we saw several crumbling sections that we had no intention of testing with our body weight. Along the sides of the road, trees grew with what I could only assume was renewed vibrancy, no longer suffering through the toxins of human pollution. Bushes and tall grasses clogged the sides, from the forest to the edge of the road, and often sprouted up onto the pavement via cracks and holes. We had an overall sense of great vulnerability. Walking was slow, zombies could appear at any time, and places for them to hide in ambush were everywhere.

We saw some people, survivors and stragglers, but they were extremely guarded. The first one made himself known to us before we saw him, signaling that we wouldn't be sneaking up on him. As an exit ramp arced its way off to our right, we saw him standing on the rise beside the highway. Crossed in his arms was a long gun. Although he was some ways away, I could feel him stare at us, unmoving, until we continued out of sight. We kept turning back, keeping an eye on him the whole time until he was hidden from view; this was someone who had *made it*. Had lived. Outside the city. It warped my mind to consider it.

No one seemed to want to make contact with us, and we felt it was best to stay out of their way, too. My God, these people had survived on their own outside the wall for years. How the hell had they done it? The mortality rate must have been sky high. We didn't see any children, but almost every person we encountered stayed their distance, eyes locked on us, and most of them showed a gun. The meaning was clear. Stay away.

Rosa and I were incredulous at these first signs of human life. We had surmised there must be someone out here, but we'd of course grown accustomed to life in the city. Living out here? It was like another world. Like those TV specials I'd seen before the outbreak, where a "lost tribe" was found on some remote island, trapped in a life generations or centuries out of date. The people we saw on the road looked completely different from us. Rather than exhibiting the sleek look of synthetic clothes and rigorous attention to cleanliness, they wore what appeared to be hand-made garments of woven fabrics and animal hides. Where our clothes were bright white or bold primary colors, theirs were subdued earthen tones: browns, greys, greens. We saw at least one man, maybe 35 years old, with a missing arm. I imagined countless ways it might've been lost, as we walked on.

Finding a relatively safe shelter at night was our biggest issue. Apartment buildings, we learned, were no good. Too many people on top of one another, making them hotbeds for infection. In one high-rise apartment building we checked out for potential shelter, we didn't find anyone alive, but had a close encounter with a zombie. It came at me unexpectedly from behind the front desk. I had to club it with my stick. His head made a cracking noise and he fell, blood spraying everywhere on the marble floor. Rosa threw up. It was traumatic for me as well, but not because of the blood. As a doctor, my promise had always been to help people. Here I was putting one down like a sick dog. Needless to say, we didn't stick around.

Our food held for the time, but we scavenged for more whenever possible. So many people had hoarded so many provisions in the early days of the disease that it was still possible to find small stashes. Mostly we weren't too hungry and avoided trouble. But spending so much time looking for food, water, and shelter made the journey slow.

Two days out from the Beltway, as we were looking for shelter for the night, our luck changed. It started to rain, darkening the bright afternoon. Our visibility diminished significantly. We scanned the area for options, then discussed what might be worth checking out. The rain must've made us hasty. We set our sights on a high school, hoping we could lock ourselves into a classroom. As we approached the school, we saw small wind turbines spinning atop the building in the increasing wind. I felt a glimmer of hope that the place might even be making electricity.

"You don't think...?" Rosa asked.

"I seriously doubt it," I said, shaking my head. "But we could always find out." *Electricity*, I let myself think, *might mean hot water.*

A side door to the school was unlocked but closed. I told myself that was a good sign. If it had been sitting wide open, I might have been more wary.

Inside, we picked a hallway at random, stood quietly listening for any signs of trouble, then opened the door to the first classroom on the right. We got about two steps in.

Looking at them, you would have thought it was a normal day of school. Eight or maybe 10 teenagers — just kids — were sitting around the classroom. After that initial false sense of security passed, I realized they were all diseased. How had they lasted in here? How had they not torn each other to bits? In the seconds before all hell broke loose, I saw that one corner of the room was a bloody mess. I guess they had turned on each other, at least once or twice, and that was how they'd survived. Maybe this had been some sort of refuge or evacuation point for them before they'd changed.

One of them, a girl with dirt-caked, blondish hair, turned toward us with milky eyes. For a heartbeat, she seemed locked in a dream. Her head swayed, milky eyes gleamed. Rain tapped its irregular beat on the cracked, grimy windows. Then lightning struck somewhere nearby, and Rosa gasped. The spell was broken. With a shriek, the girl zombie leaped up, throwing herself toward us. The others saw the focus of her rage and joined the attack. Rosa backpedaled out of the doorway, back into the hallway. I don't know what she hit, but she tripped, falling backward. I stepped back directly onto her foot, twisted my ankle trying to avoid going down myself. The girl zombie was upon me and I swung my walking stick. Her face imploded, and she fell. Even in the rush of the moment, the guilt of killing this child hit me like a brick. I *killed* someone, *again*. In an instant, my mind dreamed up the life this girl never got to live. I hated myself, our world, our lives.

But there was no time. Another zombie, a boy, bounded over the girl, came at me. I couldn't swing in time. Just before he got to me, Rosa's stick came up and took him through the throat. He fell on top of the girl, partially blocking the doorway. The other zombies scrambled to get through. I had half a second to help Rosa up, and then we ran. I realized she was crying. Down the hallway, a random left turn, hoping to put distance and a closed door between us and the infected. Hoping we could escape the chase. My ankle hurt like a son of a bitch. Rosa seemed unhurt, but she sobbed as she ran. She helped me, dragging me by the hand as fast as possible. Thankfully, we still had our sticks and backpacks.

In seconds, the other zombie kids were out in the hallway, running after us. But now their rage actually helped us. They fought each other as they tried to follow us. It slowed them down. We took two more turns at random. In the back of my mind, I hoped we wouldn't just be running into the arms of another classroom of zombies. Rosa tried three doors — two were locked, the third opened. It looked like some kind of office. We skidded inside, closed the door.

Rosa turned and half screamed. Something hit me in the back of the head, hard, and I went down in a total blackout.

11

I wasn't out long, less than a minute. It was another kid who'd hit me, but human, not zombie. Maybe 16, messy, jet-black hair, wearing a pair of threadbare jeans and a faded red t-shirt that looked washed a few thousand times more than they'd been designed to withstand. He puffed himself up in front of us, maintaining a white-knuckled grip on the metal pipe that I assumed was responsible for the growing lump on my head. A lot of bravado, but why? Then it became clear. From behind a desk, a teenage girl appeared, light red hair, freckles, adjusting the shoulder strap of her black bra under her faded light-blue blouse. Shit. Even in the freaking apocalypse, kids would be kids.

Knowing the zombies were somewhere just outside, I quietly asked, "What's your name, son?"

"What the hell are you doing here?" he responded. Looking back and forth between us and his girlfriend, switching moment by moment between strong hero and sappy boyfriend.

"Listen," I said, "we ran into some kids with the disease and they were chasing us. We didn't mean to barge in on you..."

"You didn't *barge in* on anything," he said, too abruptly.

"I honestly don't care. The world is a mess. Make yourself happy any way you can. What's your name?"

"David. David Chen." Good-looking young kid. Chinese, I figured, based on his name and appearance. Not that it mattered. These days there were only two types of people: infected and not infected. I imagined racism was finally conquered.

The girl was cute, a little pimply. "I'm Siobhan McDermott," she said. They both still looked like rats in a trap.

"You're not supposed to be here either, are you?" I asked.

After a moment, David said, "Not really." Another moment. His eyes widened. "Wait. You ran into zombies? Here in the school?" David's look of concern made it clear that was unexpected.

I studied him, trying to gauge his reaction. "You thought this place was all clear?"

"Yeah, of course — I mean, it *should* be." It was obvious that someone had told him the school was safe. And here I was, a stranger, saying maybe it wasn't.

Outside, the zombies surged past the door, searching for us. The kid's eyes bugged out. As much as he might try to be brave and in charge with his girlfriend, he was still green as hell. I guess we all were, really.

"We need to get away from here," Rosa whispered. "It's not safe."

At the back of the office, another doorway led to some unknown place. "We need to go this way," Siobhan offered, opening the door.

We followed David and Siobhan as they led us through the administrative back ways of the school. It was raining harder outside, the drumming rain punctuated by snaps of thunder and flashes of lightning. After a few dark turns, we came to another door.

For reasons we didn't then understand, David and Siobhan seemed pensive looked at each other. After a sigh, they opened the door.

12

We stepped into an alien world. In a back room next to the gymnasium, supplies were stacked high. Everything was neat and tidy. Through a glass pane, we could see into the gym. It was arranged almost like a park, with tables and chairs spread around an open space. On the sides of the large room were makeshift enclosed areas that I assumed were for privacy or sleeping or both, their contents hidden behind plywood, fabrics swaths, whatever was available. Outside, the storm raged, but inside, the large gymnasium lights made everything bright and cheerful. *Damn*, I thought, *those turbines do work*. The sight of functioning electrical lights kept my attention for another minute before I continued to look around. There were even potted plants arranged to beautify some of the spaces. Dozens of people were there — people who lived *outside* city walls — talking, laughing, playing, carrying on like life was normal. Here we were, in the land that every living soul in the walled city feared, and not only were people not living in squalor, fighting for their lives, wrestling in the grip of the disease. They were reading books, playing chess, telling stories. They were just living. It took my breath away.

For a moment, I thought, *This is The Oasis. Or if it isn't, we don't need any other.* Then we met Hector.

He stormed up to us, in a matching dark-grey athletic t-shirt and shorts, with thick, close-cropped black hair, tanned muscles bulging in a show of strength. He blocked us from entering the gym. "Are you out of your mind, David?" he asked. "Have you forgotten the rules?" Looking around, I realized the other people were mostly teenagers. Maybe four or five of them were adults, but young, barely out of their teens themselves. Hector was the oldest person we saw, and he was maybe 30. I could tell right away that he used his age as an advantage with the group. And I could tell right away that he saw me as a threat to his authority.

"They were in trouble, Hector," David said.

"Aren't we all? Every day? Every minute?" Hector sounded like he was warming up for a sermon.

"They were being chased down."

"So what?" Hector snapped. "So it's okay to jeopardize the whole group because two *complete strangers* are in trouble?"

"It's not that —"

Hector interrupted. "Yeah, it is *that*. It is exactly *that*. Here's what's going to happen. You brought them in. You're taking them out. The back door. Now, before there's more trouble."

"But —" Siobhan started.

Hector turned to her with a scoff that closed her mouth immediately. It was clear that he wasn't used to being questioned.

"We only wanted a place to sleep out of the rain tonight," I said. "Can we at least get that? We'll leave in the morning and give you no trouble."

Hector stared. I think because I wasn't speaking like a raving lunatic, he didn't know what to say at first. It didn't last long.

"Oh, and we're just supposed to *trust* that you're not infected yourself? No way. Out. Now." Hector puffed himself up as big as possible.

"We're not infected!" Rosa said.

"And just how do you know that?" Hector chided.

"Fine. We'll leave," I said. "If you can help us with one thing."

"What?" Hector's surprise was obvious.

"You know this area, I assume. It's raining like hell out there. You must know some place close by where we can shelter for the night."

Hector thought about it. He seemed very reluctant to give up any information. Everyone was silent, looking back and forth at one another for a moment.

"The supply shed. Behind the bleachers." It was David who spoke up. "It stays dry, and we've been in there, so we know there aren't any zombies."

Hector put on a sour expression for effect and to maintain his air of control, but acquiesced. "One night," he said. "And you go there now."

In minutes we stood at the back door, gauging the rain and the best route to run to the shed. David pointed the way. "Sorry for, you know, knocking you in the head."

"Don't worry about it, kid. Thanks for trying to help us." I looked back at the gym, the warm beds and bright lights and plentiful supplies, and gave a regretful sigh. And we ran into the rain. The distance was maybe a few hundred yards, enough for us to get pretty soaked on the way. The shed was large and dry, but not built for comfort. As the storm intensified outside, we slept on the concrete slab floor. In the end, it may have saved our lives, despite the hours we spent shivering in our cold, damp clothes.

* * *

The next morning the rain had stopped. We awoke, ate some canned food from our provisions, and started back toward the highway. As we went past the gymnasium, a door flung open and Hector appeared. He ran toward us. He was holding a pistol.

"You killed them!" he shouted. Others piled out behind him, including David and Siobhan.

"It's not their fault!" David yelled, pushing past people to get to Hector.

Shocked by the scene, I stood in place as Hector approached. It was one part fear that running would mean a bullet in my back, one part good old-fashioned inaction in the face of danger. Hector charged right up to me and trained the pistol on my forehead.

"What the hell is going on?" I asked quietly. Beside me Rosa gasped and leapt forward. Hector slid the pistol over toward her and she stopped short. He pointed it back to me.

"Last night," Hector panted. "Because of you, we were attacked. Zombies *everywhere*. Goddammit. We were holed up all night. We ended up killing all the damn things — 23 of them. Eight of my people *died*. Just because you had to show up." He cocked the pistol. From what we saw the day before, there were only 30 or 40 people living there in the first place. The community had gotten a heck of a lot smaller in one night.

"Hector!" Siobhan shouted. "She's dead. This won't bring her back." Hector paused, and the pistol dipped a bit. Then he raised it in fury, back at my head.

"Please. Anna wouldn't want *this*." Siobhan extended her hand for the gun. I could only guess who Anna was. Hector's wife or girlfriend or mother or sister. The specifics didn't matter at the moment.

Wheeling around, Hector changed his focus. "Actually, I suppose it was *you two* who are really responsible." He looked toward David and Siobhan. "Pack up your things, you're out of here today."

Siobhan stepped back. "No! We'll die outside!"

I looked at Hector, into his eyes. He was on the edge, maybe on the edge of sanity. Anything could happen.

Quickly, he shifted the pistol's aim and fired, three fast shots, chest, shoulder, face. Siobhan dropped, dead. David leaped on top of Hector and they fell, rolling and fighting. Everyone scattered. The gun went off again, once, twice. If this was The Oasis, it was crumbling. There was nothing we could do to fix it. We ran.

KEITH SOARES

13

Interstate 95 runs up and down the entire East Coast, connecting most of the big cities. In between long stretches of pavement sided by nothing but trees, there were clusters of strip malls and office developments sitting along the highway. If you couldn't find it along 95, you couldn't find it anywhere. We weren't really looking for anything in particular, except food and nightly shelter, but then we saw it: an RV dealership. The sign promised comfortable living and happy families traveling across the country. The appeal was instantly overwhelming: our own vehicle, to make the travel faster, to carry our gear, to keep us out of bad weather... and most importantly, to sleep in safely every night. Unfortunately, we weren't the only people to think that. The dealership was pretty much cleaned out. There were a couple of huge vehicles left, but peering through the window I could see I didn't have a clue how to drive them. There was a pickup truck with a camper trailer, but that would mean two separate, self-contained spaces to worry about — the truck cockpit and the camper interior. Around back, we got lucky, coming across a smallish integrated RV that might have been the owners' private ride. It was locked. Rosa went to the dealership office and tried the door. It, too, was locked, so she broke a small window, reached through, and let herself in. She had to step over a dead body, desiccated beyond recognition, with wisps of clothing and the last remnants of skin and hair clinging to its greyish form. She tried drawers and cabinets, and ended up with a ridiculous number of keys. Back at the RV, she tried nearly every one until finally the door opened, and she jumped into the driver's seat.

"Okay, now what?" she asked.

I checked the tires and found them in passable condition. "Do you know how to drive one of these things?" I asking, moving over to look at the range of dials and controls in front of her.

"I don't know how to drive. Period. I never got a license because I lived in the city." Rosa smirked.

"I used to drive a 'luxury sedan,'" I said. "That seems like another lifetime." Rosa hopped out and I got behind the wheel. I put the key in the ignition and turned it. Nothing.

"When I was a teenager, my parents made me learn a little bit about cars," I said as I reached under the dashboard, looking for the hood release. I pulled it, and the RV's hood popped free with a *kachunk*. I moved to the front of the RV. "I'm thinking it's the battery. I doubt it could sit here for 10 years, or even just a few years, depending on the last time it ran." I opened the hood and there was the dead battery, mottled with corrosion, mocking me.

"What do we do?" Rosa asked.

"Well, two ideas come to mind. First, we push this baby over to a downhill slope and hope that we can pop the clutch and get 'er started." I could tell that my sarcasm was lost on Rosa, the non-driver. "But given that this is an automatic transmission, that's out of the question."

She peered at me from the driver's side window. "Plan B?"

"I have a thin hope that our RV dealer friend was also into disaster preparation. Let's look around." We went back to the office and dug around, then wandered through a door and into a small workroom. Looking carefully, I found something I hadn't seen in several decades: a trickle battery charger. I put it on a countertop. I found some tools and was able to disconnect the battery from the RV and bring it back into the workshop, where I placed it next to the charger. I headed back outside with increased purpose, and followed the outer edge of the building. Tucked in a back corner where most people would never look, there was a thicket of overgrown bushes.

Underneath I saw the glint of metal and began pulling away the leaves and branches, revealing an old gas generator tied into the office building.

With a rush of excitement, I ran back to the workroom and rummaged about, eventually coming up with a small gas canister and a hose. Back at the RV, I prayed there was enough gas inside for us to steal some, then opened the tank, inserted the hose, and placed the canister on the ground. Pushing the hose inward, I heard a liquid *spoosh*. My heart raced. Rosa looked at me like I had gone mad. In my haste, I'd neglected to tell her anything about what I was doing. Now I put the loose end of the hose in my mouth and sucked. I jammed the hose into the canister and after a second watched as it filled with a clear brown liquid. Gasoline, thank God, pouring into the canister. I tried my best to estimate how much it would take to power up the generator and get some charge on the battery, while still leaving enough to drive the RV. In the end, as a total guess, I siphoned off maybe two-thirds of a gallon of gas.

Next I had to worry about the generator. I brushed it off and opened the screw top to the fuel tank. Delicately, I poured the gas into the opening, splashing a few times, cursing my jittery old hands. With the canister dry, I had a quiet, almost desperate moment of reckoning. I closed the screw top, reached for the pull chain to start the engine. "Wish me luck," I said, winking at Rosa.

"Luck," she said drably.

I pulled. Nothing.

I pulled again. Nothing but the slightest sluggish whir. I checked the choke, thanking my parents silently for insisting that I know something about this when I was young. Pulled it open. Tugged again. Nothing. Once more. A little rumble. Hope sprang. Again I pulled, feeling the strain already in my shoulder and arm. The motor sputtered, coughed, almost gave up... and then ran so high I thought it might blow. Rosa stepped back, surprised. Remembering something else about the choke, I rushed to push it in, almost too quickly. The engine slowed, came near to stall, but finally evened out. I looked at Rosa, unbelieving. A wide grin spread across my face, and she couldn't help but follow suit. Then I ran back inside. "Are you going to tell me what you're doing?" she yelled.

In the workroom, I flicked on the light switch, checking for power, but nothing came on. In the fading light of day, I saw the bulb was missing from the overhead fixture. I'd have to leave it to luck. I plugged in the battery charger, turned a switch. A tiny red light appeared, and I laughed out loud. "We're going to charge this battery!" I was giddy. "Or, well, I *hope* we are. If the gas holds out." I connected the battery to the charger, checked the gauges. It really did seem to be working.

"How long does it take?" Rosa asked, peering over my shoulder.

My smile faded. "That's the problem. This is a trickle charger. It's called that because it trickles the charge into the battery a little bit at a time. My guess is, as much as eight hours."

"Eight hours?" she asked. "You really think that little bit of gas will last that long? And what do we do in the meantime?"

"I guess we wait."

* * *

We holed up in the workroom, afraid that the noise from the generator might attract undue attention. It was a nervous night, but we finally dozed. It must have been around three or four o'clock in the morning when something suddenly woke us up. It was silence.

"What happened?" Rosa asked, groggy but wary.

"The generator died. Ran out of fuel."

"Now what?" Her eyes looked at me in confusion, hope, tiredness.

"In the morning, we try it out."

* * *

As the morning light filtered in, I unhooked the battery and grabbed a tool. From the office, I peered out the window to make sure the coast was clear. It was. Carefully, I walked to the RV and reconnected the battery. If this failed, the idea of trudging on foot another day made me feel so weary I couldn't move. I looked at Rosa, nodding for her to try the key. Though she didn't drive, she understood. She sat in the driver's seat and turned the ignition.

Somehow, the engine started. I rushed over and checked the fuel gauge: less than a quarter tank. A lot less. That was going to be a problem. We'd need to make finding fuel a priority, on top of finding food. We let the engine run, wasting gas but further charging the battery. Using the canister and hose, we checked all the other vehicles we could find on the lot and came up with another gallon and a half of gas, which we poured straight into the RV's tank. Then it was time to check out the rest of the RV's interior. What a lucky break. It was totally tricked out. Here we were in the ruins of civilization, and we would be driving an RV with leather seats, a refrigerator, stove, bed, even a bathroom. And it was clean. That was a relief after days of living in conditions that life behind the wall had taught us to fear. We didn't talk about it, but I'm sure Rosa was as afraid as I was that we might be exposing ourselves to the disease. The RV was tidy, and a place we could reasonably keep clean by ourselves.

* * *

Rosa was interested in learning how to drive. I found that I reacquainted myself with driving pretty quickly, and so I taught her. It was easy, since the car was an automatic. And it didn't hurt that there was a complete lack of other cars on the road. We had to navigate around potholes, frequent pileups, and abandoned cars, but that mostly just broke up the boredom of the drive. The freedom and exhilaration of driving was just about the most fun thing we had done in years.

All of the gas stations we checked were bone dry, so when we stopped to scavenge for food, we also looked for smaller stashes of gas. Given the state of the world, the desperate, aborted migrations that followed the disease, there were a lot of junked cars with spare gas cans in the trunk. We hoarded these and were able to fill up the tank. The small RV got decent gas mileage — about 24 miles per gallon — but even still, with 500 miles or so to go, we'd need more than 20 gallons. And that was assuming our destination was where we thought it was.

While scavenging, we also topped off the RV's water tank and loaded up the refrigerator and cabinets with anything remotely edible that we could find. We checked stores and houses near the RV dealership and off the next few exits along 95. With water and food, and a brand-new moving shelter loaded with a full tank of gas, we felt great.

Before we hit the road in earnest, I decided to try out the toilet, but wanted to be sure it worked first. The toilet fed into a tank labeled Black Water. I found out, much to my dismay, that it was already partially full. We decided the rest of the world wouldn't mind too much if we simply let the toilet drain out onto the road.

After all, we'd been doing our business outside since we began the trip. We doubted anyone would mind too much.

* * *

Having spent most of the day searching for supplies to fill the RV, we made little progress on the road, and the tension of the previous night made us tired early. As dusk settled in, we found a place to stop, on an overpass where we could see every approaching direction fairly well. We decided to get some sleep. Rosa went to the back while I locked up the RV and shut down the engine. I turned to go back to where the bed was located... and stopped. In the fading light, I saw Rosa slip out of her worn shirt and pants, standing in her underwear, her lean, olive-toned body reflecting the sun in warm curves. She looked up and paused, her eyes on mine.

I noticed I was holding my breath. "Uh... sorry," I said, turning and taking in air.

After a pause, I heard her say, "Don't worry." She got into the bed and turned toward me. "There's only one bed. We've slept side-by-side each night now. It's okay."

I looked at her, then looked around the RV.

"Come. Lie down. Here."

So I did.

14

We made great time all the way through to Richmond. But we had to be careful once we got there — last we heard, Richmond was a functional, walled city, like DC. We continued on 95, driving straight toward its heart. As we approached the Route 1 overpass, we saw that the space between the bridge and the street below had been filled in, walling off the entrance. Cars and trucks were heaped along the shoulders of the road, like they had been deliberately swept aside to clear the way. It was impossible to tell if the fortifications were guarded; if anyone still kept up the city's defenses. Rosa drove ahead. Slowly, carefully.

A blast tore open the ground just ahead, to the passenger side of the RV, with a sound loud enough to cancel out everything else and leave my ears ringing. My nose filled with an acrid smell. Tiny bits of pavement rained onto the RV. Rosa swerved left, more a flinching move than actual defensive driving, sending me flailing toward into the passenger door. The RV wasn't moving all that quickly, but it was tall and the turn was sudden. For a moment we skittered up on two wheels before thudding back down to the road, Rosa zigging to try to regain control. The RV slammed against a low concrete wall dividing the two sides of the highway and dragged to a stop, throwing sparks.

Rosa turned to look at me. "What the hell was — ?" Another shot missed overhead, cutting into an abandoned car in the opposite lane. There must have been some gas left in its tank; the car jumped into the air in a fireball explosion, making a low *whump*.

"Go!" I shouted. "Back the way we came! Turn us around!"

With a ripping of metal on concrete, Rosa drove forward. She had to get off the wall before she could turn around. "How far can they shoot?" she asked.

"I have no idea, just keep going!" Somehow she turned the RV around. Another blast, now behind us, lifted our back end. For a moment, it looked like the extra push of the explosion would send us crashing directly into a pickup truck that angled out from the side of the highway.

At the last minute, Rosa swerved. I was sure that I hadn't taught her anything like that. I think it was just her good instincts. Then she did something even smarter. She drove toward the shoulder, where a large tractor-trailer jutted diagonally into the road. She put it between us and the city wall, buying us the seconds we needed. As I looked back, I saw the barrel of the mounted gun — a huge thing, I have no idea what to even call it — turning to aim at us again. But as Rosa sped away, it didn't fire.

Maybe we were out of range, maybe we no longer appeared to be a threat, or maybe they just wanted to conserve ammunition. Either way, we lived.

15

We backtracked north for a few miles, passing several exits, before I finally asked Rosa to pull off at an interchange where it looked like we might be able to find supplies. After several wasted stops, we came across a convenience store a couple of turns off the main road that ended up being a great find — a storeroom held food, water, a small can of gas, and something we suddenly realized we really needed: a map. We vowed not to venture into the big cities again.

Using the map, we realized we could skirt around Richmond using 295 — we hoped it would swing wide enough to avoid any future confrontations. It did.

The RV was scuffed up on the driver's side and the mirror was broken off, but it didn't seem like we'd have to look behind us for too much other traffic, and we weren't terribly concerned about having the nicest car on the road. It still handled fine. Rosa had had enough driving for one day, and passed the job to me. Soon, she was napping in the passenger seat while I navigated around Richmond.

The rest of the drive through Virginia was uneventful, except for one moment in a remote, densely wooded section of the highway. Out of nowhere, a zombie ran directly into the road. Rosa startled awake as we clipped him with the passenger side of the RV, no doubt denting up that side of the vehicle, too. She screamed. I tried to defuse the tension. "The way we drive, they may take our license away," I said. She just stared at the blood that was dripping down the passenger window next to her.

* * *

Driving into North Carolina seemed like a huge accomplishment. First, we had been in Virginia since the moment we landed the paddleboats coming out of DC. And second, it just *felt* closer to South Carolina, our objective.

Just past the border, I had to pee, so we pulled over and I went to use the small bathroom in the RV. Rosa, seeming morbidly fascinated by the bloody mess on the passenger side of the car, got out to take a look. Afterward, I guessed that the combination of our vehicle approaching, doors opening and closing, and other sounds of human activity must have stirred up interest. A zombie we might otherwise have dismissed as a corpse on the side of the road stood, shook itself free of the underbrush, and made directly for Rosa. From inside the bathroom, I heard her shout. My heart raced, and I fumbled my way outside as fast as possible.

There, my racing heart almost stopped.

A frantic zombie was on top of Rosa, who'd fallen to the street, backpedaling desperately with her elbows and feet, trying for some purchase to get away. The zombie, formerly a dark-skinned woman, perhaps 50 years old, somewhat overweight, scrambled to keep Rosa down, to bite and tear at her.

I turned, flung open the tire compartment at the rear of the RV, and grabbed whatever I could. It was a small jack for replacing a flat tire. I didn't care. It was metal and heavy. I hefted it, and ran.

My only thought was: *Let her be okay*. Skidding up behind the zombie, I cocked my arm and hit the thing as hard as I could. The zombie woman didn't just fall, she was launched to the side of Rosa in a splatter of blood and gore. I stopped, looked at the zombie, ready to do it again. She didn't move. Given the state of her skull, I figured she'd never move again.

Rosa was up on her elbows, looking down at herself. She was incredulous, shocked. No, horrified. Following her eyes, I saw why.

Her shirt had a vertical tear, and under that it was clear that the zombie had slashed her across the belly.

As she slowly looked up at me, anguish in her eyes, the zombie's blood and her own continued to mix in the wound. It felt like the cut continued down into my core, my soul.

A tear opened between us, and the part of me that Rosa had become was ripped away.

16

She lived. We had no idea if it would be for long or for short, but damn it, she was alive. We would continue south, come what may. The journey took on even greater urgency. Where before, I had come along on this quest for The Oasis out of duty to Rosa, now it took on much more serious weight. I began to feel that I had to get her to The Oasis or she would turn into a zombie in front of my eyes. It was all I had to hold on to; they might shun us, they might have no way to help her, hell, they probably didn't even *exist*, but there was nothing else. No other option.

We had a good-sized first-aid kit in the RV, and I patched her up, wiping everything as clean as I could. But it was a pale comparison to what we'd known for the last 10 years. Life in DC was infinitely more sterile than the half-assed roadside clean up I was able to provide. Still, it would have to do.

Now I thundered down the highway, willing us to get to our destination as soon as we could. We tore through North Carolina — it was nothing but a blur to me. Rosa faded in and out of consciousness. The biggest concern I had was Fayetteville, which was the largest city near the highway, a potential bottleneck, possibly even a walled-off dead end. But we raced past the city like it was a ghost town. How many hundreds of thousands of people had lived in Fayetteville? I guess most of them were dead now. The futility of my every move felt like an anchor around my neck.

I'd reviewed the map we found, and knew that around Florence, South Carolina, I had to finally get off 95 and head west on Interstate 20. That would take us right past Columbia. I hoped not too close.

In the end, we covered hundreds of miles in a blink. We probably were the noisiest thing in the entire (former) state of South Carolina. From any other vantage point, I must have looked insane. Perhaps even diseased. I was driving as fast as possible down highways blasted with potholes, a never-ending boneyard of cars in various states of disrepair, rust, collision damage, fire damage. And our luxury RV was zipping in and out of lanes, trying to make time.

Interstate 20 was a blur. I guess we were wide enough of Columbia to avoid trouble, or maybe we came and went so fast they didn't have time to react. Rosa got a little better; at least she woke up. I could sense the pain and fear clearly etched across my face, knew she could see it, but she looked oddly calm. Like all was well, all was at peace... or perhaps, all was coming to an end.

Using the map, Rosa, her voice a whisper, guided me into an expanse of lakes and parks along the South Carolina–Georgia border. My heart dropped again, seeing the large swath of green on the paper map — it seemed impossibly huge to search. Even if The Oasis was there, could we find it in time for them to do something for Rosa? But studying the lakes, parks, and roads, she had a hunch, and directed me to Hickory Knob State Park, and damn if she wasn't right. We found them. Because they weren't hiding from anyone. The compound was right there, on the shore of Clarks Hill Lake. Makeshift but solid-looking walls blocked off the road. As we pulled near and stopped, dozens of people came out. They met us beside the golf course. Some people were even out playing golf. The idea was absurd, and knowing nothing of the game, I looked at them like they were from another planet. I saw that some of the people approaching us were carrying guns, but for the most part they all just looked curious. A small girl waved in welcome. They were alive. They were just people. And they were right where Rosa had said they would be. I turned and beamed at her, in awe of her brilliance. In the entire wide world, she had found The Oasis.

Rosa and I hugged, sobbing, for a long time.

17

They could tell right away that something bad had happened to Rosa. She was pale, her breathing shallow, and the large wrap of bandages on her stomach was seeping blood. Strangely, they didn't do what we expected; they didn't shut us out, shun us, run us away. Rosa had the disease and we all knew it, yet the people of The Oasis did... *nothing*.

A young woman stepped forward. "Where are you from?" she asked.

"DC," Rosa said, her voice weaker than I was used to hearing.

"Well, you're here now. We don't live that way, the way they do in the cities." No declaration of arrival to the hallowed Oasis. "I'm Caroline."

Rosa stretched to shake Caroline's hand, but winced in pain from the injury to her mid-section. Caroline turned to the older man next to her. "We need to see Harvey," she said.

"I hope you live," said a young voice. It was the little girl who had waved to us.

"Eva, shush," said Caroline. Turning to us, she added, "Kids overreact."

Behind them, the gate blocking the road rolled open. For a brief moment, I thought I had just traded one walled city for another, and wondered why. I felt a moment of fear. It wouldn't be the last.

"You'd be better off driving up," Caroline said, looking at Rosa's bandages. I nodded. Caroline and two others climbed into a pickup truck just inside the gate. It was the first time we'd seen another moving vehicle on our trip. The oddness of it struck me.

Back in the RV, it seemed almost like a victory lap — one last moment in our home on wheels. I hoped it wasn't a last moment for Rosa entirely.

At the end of a small spit of land jutting into the lake, the road blossomed into a wide, sweeping loop. Inside the loop a huge building loomed, austere brick with wide, white-paned windows opening on the lake. Additional smaller buildings, similar in style, with brick and large windows, stretched off to the side, and there were even tennis courts and a pool. I felt like I was in a dream, seeing the way they lived out here in the wild. Around the grounds, individual homes made neat rows; these had the appearance of being built more recently. Outside the looping drive, tents appeared scattered through the woods. I assumed we weren't the only stragglers to find our way here. There was a parking lot at the end of the road. Several well-maintained cars and trucks were parked there, but many spaces remained open. The pickup parked in one of them. Caroline guided us into another space, and she and her friends helped Rosa out of the RV. Together we all walked to the large main building.

It was called the Hickory Knob State Park Lodge, and we were told it offered 76 rooms and its own restaurant. The restaurant was bustling as we walked in, although people turned and stared at our unfamiliar faces. My first impression of the building being a huge home for one important family — heightened by the sense that we were being taken to their leader — was way off. This was more commune than palace.

Nevertheless, we *were* taken to their leader, Harvey. He was an older, rather disheveled man, with a comb-over hairstyle to hide his mostly bald head. Ten years into the disease, and small vanities still prevailed. His natural posture seemed to be a sort of half-stoop, accented by a heavy-set build and sloppy, rumpled clothes. He stood up from a tiny, plain desk in the small office behind the lobby counter, walked over to us, and put out his hand. "I'm Harvey," was all he said.

The place was... well, it was filthy. We had grown used to a certain amount of unclean on the road, but still held ourselves to the sterile standards of the city. *Stay clean, stay alive.* But not here. If this was The Oasis, it was The Oasis of Filth. I was stunned. Rosa seemed too ill to care, but I saw it. It was so different from our lives behind the wall, even from our lives in the RV, that it was shocking. Things were *not* pristine. Things were *not* scoured clean. Had we just traveled hundreds of miles, risked everything, only to expose ourselves to the disease here? But these people. They looked healthy, even happy. How did they do it? They must have some answer.

"We need your help," I said.

"Hold on, now. Where're you from?" Harvey cocked his head.

"She's been infected."

I swear he rolled his eyes. "I know. Where are you from?"

"DC. Come on! She's infected!"

"And you brought her here anyway?" Harvey asked.

What else could I say? "I thought The Oasis was her only hope."

"You were probably right. And stupid as hell." Harvey was crass, but seemed to be very smart. I stared at him. Was this wise, or the stupidest thing I'd ever do?

"Help her," I finally said, tilting my head down as a wave of exhaustion set in. His eyebrows raised.

"You think we *can* help her?" he asked, eyeing Rosa's condition, her bandages tinted pink.

"Yes."

"Why?"

"I... I have no idea. But there has to be some reason. A reason why I met her. A reason why she knew you were here. A reason we got here when we did."

Harvey scoffed. "I haven't found much of life works with reason."

"But you can help her?"

107

He paused. "Probably... but you have to do it our way."

"I don't know of any other way," I said.

One last sweeping look, to judge me, I guessed. To judge *us*. Then his expression changed. He became very businesslike. "Then we should move quickly. She won't last." Harvey turned to look at the people around him. A glance, a nod, then they were all set.

They took us back outside, led us to a private cottage. Its front porch was made of wood, knotty and comfortably worn, and held rocking chairs that begged to be used in the afternoon warmth. We stepped past all that. The front door was open.

We walked inside. Rosa coughed, stumbled. She ended up on her knees on the floor. I moved to help her, but was held back. The cottage's lobby looked like it was wrapped completely in plastic. Two people grabbed my arms from behind and dragged me away. I saw Rosa, seemingly unconscious, being carried in another direction.

"Rosa!" I shouted. She was taken into a room with bright lights. The door closed and she was gone. I figured I would never see her again.

18

They took me to a similar bright room, and just like the lobby, it was covered in plastic. "What the hell are you doing to us? Let me go!" I shouted, with no results. The two burly young men in light-blue medical garb who were holding my arms took me to a hospital gurney in the middle of the room. I struggled, but they easily strapped me down, then left the room. I was lined up next to another gurney, where another person lay strapped down. The whole trip, the whole idea of The Oasis, was a huge joke. They must be taking in stragglers off the streets for some perverse game.

Thinking that the person next to me — a man, I could see, maybe 25 or 30 — was someone who must have wandered into their grasp, too, I tried to make eye contact. And I realized he was really, really sick.

He looked feverish, nearly unconscious. I remembered Noah, sweating on that first cool day. These people had just strapped me down next to a soon-to-be-zombie. Was this their idea of fun? Maybe they'd watch as he turned, then tore at his straps until he was free to come rip me apart. All that plastic would make for easy clean up.

Why hadn't we been more cautious? Rosa, well, she just believed. And I was desperate to get her help. It was a pair of fatal mistakes.

The door opened again, and Harvey walked in.

"You son of a bitch!" I started. He just held up his two large hands in front of him, calmly.

"Hold on," he said. "I know how this looks."

"Really? Because to me, it looks like you're about to watch us die, for sport!" Harvey seemed confused. Then he turned to look at the other gurney, and my meaning dawned on him.

"Oh." His eyes got slightly wider. "Oh. You think — well." He stammered, but also seemed amused. If I could have ripped him limb from limb at that moment, I would have.

He leaned over me, eyes darting around, checking everything over. "This is going to be really unpleasant for you, I won't lie." Then he did crack a small smile. "But not in the way you think. The man next to you is named Todd. But he *doesn't* have the disease. He has the *flu*." Harvey turned and walked out, and a nurse came in, dressed all in white, a strange reminder of Terry Rawlins, my nurse before the disease.

She took my vital signs without a word. Then she prepped a small rolling cart carrying a tray stacked with instruments. To my surprise, she pushed it over next to the other man, Todd. After a brief check of his vitals and a few marks on a chart that hung off the end of his gurney, she raised a long, thin, wooden stick with a cotton swab on the end. Peeling Todd's lips apart, she twirled the cotton swab in his mouth, covering it with his saliva. Then she turned to me.

She reached for my mouth, and a combination of terror and revulsion went through me in a fast wave. "No! Stop that — leave me alone!" I turned my head away. Her latex-gloved hand reached out, grabbed my chin. She was strong and clearly used to these feeble attempts to ward her off. She leaned over me while tipping my head back, and managed to open my lips with her fingers. I was desperate. I tried to thrash my head back and forth. I may even have snapped my teeth at her fingers to make her back away. It was all pointless. She stuck the cotton swab into my mouth, and Todd's saliva mixed with mine. I had the urge to throw up. Instead, I spat at her, hitting her in the face. She flinched, but only slightly, then turned and methodically cleaned up herself, her tray and instruments. She tossed the cotton swab in a trash container in the corner of the room, and left without another glance in my direction.

19

Her name was Marian. She was 56, Caucasian, a mix of English and German in her family tree. She was about five-foot-10, and built solid — a battle-axe, someone my age might have called her. She'd been a nurse in Augusta before the outbreak, and remained one afterward until the city fell. She didn't know where to go once the walls came down, but in that part of the country the rumors about The Oasis were more persistent, and much more specific. She joined a caravan heading north. Harvey was impressed with her right away and, after her own processing, asked her to help with The Oasis' medical staff. She was pragmatic. She knew what had to be done and knew she could do it. Now here she was, processing Rosa and me.

Processing was the official welcoming procedure for anyone arriving at The Oasis. It was standard for them not to tell you what it was until they got you started. Marian told me that they used to try to be nice and explain it up front, but too many people refused to do it then still wanted to stay. So Harvey declared, and the residents of The Oasis agreed, that everyone who wanted to stay had to be processed. A couple of the ones who refused turned belligerent. There was some bloodshed. But processing continued, and The Oasis stayed safe.

I had a lot of time on my hands. Eventually, after three or four episodes with the cotton swab, two men rolled Todd out, and I stayed by myself. I started to feel sick, but in a more *normal* sense — sore throat, fever, aches and pains. It felt... old-fashioned. They'd obviously given me the flu by introducing Todd's germs into my system. Marian kept me hydrated and regularly checked my vitals, marking them down on my chart.

I learned that it all started as an accident. Before there was The Oasis, when the first dozen or so people came to Hickory Knob State Park Lodge, looking for refuge, two of them were in the very beginning stages of the flu. The two men had been chicken farmers, and the common theory later on was that they'd contracted a strain of avian flu. As the others began to notice their symptoms, the group fractured. The majority wanted to send the two men away, fearing they were becoming zombies and would infect everyone. One person objected: Harvey. He was just one of the group then, not a leader, but he was just as forceful, just as brash, and wouldn't let them condemn the others to die. He volunteered to take the sick men to a small building and take care of them. And that's how he became the first processing nurse of the community that grew into The Oasis. Under Harvey's care, the men got better in a few days. Then Harvey himself became ill, and the people who had railed against his plan said it was fate, that even if he had been able somehow to save the two men, now he himself would become a zombie. But he didn't. Harvey's wife, Anne, was one of the original members of the group and couldn't just let him die, and so she entered the building and served as his nurse, caring for him until he got better. In a just over a week, when they felt certain it was over, Harvey opened the doors of the small building where he'd first taken the two chicken farmers and walked out, with the two men behind him. All three were well. The rest of the group was forced to readmit them, but remained wary. Anne contracted the flu and remained in quarantine, with Harvey nursing her to return the favor.

A few days later, there was trouble. Back then, The Oasis didn't have any fortifications, just the lodge itself. And given its size, they hadn't been able to check out the entire complex. With the flu outbreak seeming to have passed, they finally went through every room, closet, office, basement, and workroom in the lodge and the surrounding buildings. After going through most of the spaces with no problem, they became a little careless. They stumbled onto a group of zombies locked into a lodge room, and were overrun. Hearing the melee, Harvey ran to help and was bitten. Three others also became infected by bites and cuts — including one of the men Harvey had nursed through the flu — before the zombies were dispatched. In time, the group watched as all four began to show signs of the disease, and began making plans to execute them. And that's when they saw that Harvey and the other man who'd just had the flu actually got *better*. As the two others continued to turn, Harvey got an idea.

He rushed the infected men to the small building and into the room with Anne. Others shouted that he was crazy, that he would kill his own wife. But he wiped mucus from Anne onto the two men, took them into another room, strapped them down, and waited.

They lived.

* * *

I asked Marian about Rosa all the time, and Marian told me she was having a rough time. The disease was already working its way through her by the time we got to The Oasis, and the processing was adding even more stress to her body. But Marian thought she would make it. During the time Rosa and I were being processed, during the deepest part of our illnesses, other new people were brought in and strapped to gurneys next to us, and they began their own processing, kicking and screaming. It was a cycle that couldn't be broken, strung out in a chain all the way back to those first two men and their avian flu.

In a week, I was released. Rosa came out four days after that. And she was fine, with no signs of the disease. Somehow the flu had saved her.

So that was why The Oasis seemed so filthy. They didn't care anymore about keeping every spot clean, of scouring every nook and corner. They just lived. A little dirt was okay when you knew you weren't risking zombie infection.

Rosa became obsessed. She'd spent years trying to find any clue that might help eradicate the disease to no avail, and now here was clear evidence of a cure, right in front of her. She asked for as many details as she could from The Oasis' processing team. Marian told her that they had to keep a live culture of the flu at all times or it wouldn't work. They tried preserving it but didn't really have any idea how to do that, which meant a constant cycle of people had to come into The Oasis and be processed. If there was any lull and no living person carried the flu to the next person, the chain would be broken and the cure would vanish forever. Rosa dove right into the middle of it, setting up a makeshift lab.

As far as I know, she only took one break that whole time, other than eating, going to the bathroom, and sleeping. She came and saw me. She looked nervous, which was uncharacteristic. "Hey, what's wrong?" I asked, trying to get her to look into my eyes.

She wouldn't make eye contact, and for a time I thought she might turn and hurry back the lab. Then she put her hand in her pocket. "I just..." she stammered.

"What?" I said, as compassionately as I could. "Look, we've been through just about everything together. Whatever you have to say, just *say it.*" Finally she looked at me. When her hand came out of her pocket, it was holding something tightly.

"I just wanted to say *thank you.* And... I made you this." She opened her hand. Inside, there was a thin, multi-colored twist of strings. She reached out, lifted my hand, and began to tie them like a band about my wrist. I looked down at her hands as she did it, and saw she still wore her colorful bracelet from her days in D.C. Where hers was made of bright synthetic fabric, mine used organic strings, cottons of various colors. I could only guess she collected them from around The Oasis. When she was finished, she pulled back a few inches to look. And we stood there, each with a colorful thin bracelet, different but still matching.

"I don't know what to say... I —" She interrupted me by quickly leaning in and placing a short, delicate kiss on my lips. I felt nothing but an electric sensation of surprise. Just as quickly, she turned and rushed out, back to her lab.

* * *

Harvey was thrilled to have a true medical researcher in the group, and so he fully supported Rosa's work. She was given access to anything and anyone she wanted. She took samples from everyone being processed. Eventually, she needed more equipment. Marian thought Augusta would be the answer — there were several hospital labs back there. The Oasis had scouting groups that routinely went out for supplies, so Harvey had Rosa make a list. She did, and even drew pictures of certain items. The scouts — a wiry young brunette with a long, braided ponytail named Janine, and a tall, muscled Korean kid named Hank — pored over her requests. Their reply: "No."

"What do you mean, no?" Rosa asked.

"No offense, but, these drawings... they're terrible." Hank pointed down at Rosa's sketches. "I wouldn't trust us to get the right thing."

Janine held out one of the pictures. "This round thing. Is this a plate? Or a ball?"

"It's a Petri dish!" Rosa shouted, throwing up her hands. "I wrote *Petri* right next to it! As many as you can get."

"Can't read your writing," Janine said with a grimace. "Sorry."

Hank was holding one of the other sketches. "What is *agar*? And would any kind of microscope work?"

"It's a solution for growing cultures... and.... Look. Never mind. I'll go." We all turned to Rosa, wide-eyed.

Harvey objected. "Now look, I know you've been out there, but you haven't been a scout and you haven't been to Augusta. Besides..." He stared at her with a serious look tinged with what seemed like... fear. "You're our only hope to truly fix this. I can't risk sending you."

She thought about that. "No. You can't risk *not* sending me. These two," gesturing at Hank and Janine, "will try their best, but they might fail. They'll *probably* fail. Then what? I make some more sketches and send them again? That's time wasted that we don't have. If we miss this window, if the virus dies out now, we may never — the *world* may never — have this chance *ever* again." She let the idea hang in the air like the fetid smell of a rotting corpse.

"Fine." Harvey was a practical man, after all.

"Me, too," I added.

Now it was time for the scouts to object. "What? Come on, but aren't you a little..."

"Old? Yeah. But I go with Rosa."

"He does," she added.

In the end, they couldn't object and still get what we all needed. So Rosa and I joined Janine and Hank on a mission to Augusta.

* * *

The next morning, we set out. Hank and Janine had a jeep fully outfitted for their scouting runs, but we had to take out some items to make room for us in the back seats. As we drove off, I looked at the boxes piled on the ground, and hoped we weren't going to need anything we left behind.

"What's in there?" I asked, gesturing back at the discarded boxes.

"Mostly grenades," Janine shouted back as the car accelerated and wind whipped around us, muffling every other sound. Hank nodded to the two young men holding open the gate as we drove through, then raced along the twisty wooded roads, headed first east, then south, taking us through the coniferous woodlands down to US

378. From studying maps before we set out, we knew that our options here were to turn left toward McCormick or right to cross the bridge into Georgia. Hank turned left without a pause.

"After the outbreak, the bridges were pretty much the first thing the military took out, especially around the walled cities," Janine said, pointing at the map. "The bridge here over the lake is still intact, but farther south we'd have to cross the reservoir on 47, and that bridge is long gone."

We rolled into McCormick not long after that. Rosa and I were shocked by what we saw.

"Did a tornado go through here or something?" Rosa asked. "Why is this town... *flat?*"

As Hank steered into town, he pointed to an abandoned bulldozer. "Harvey's orders. See that bulldozer? We used that and a couple other ones to tear everything down. McCormick isn't much, but it's the closest town to camp and we saw zombies in the area. Harvey thought it would be safest to just run the place into the ground, so there was nowhere for them to hide." Hank turned right onto Mine Street, aiming south again. A few blocks along, I looked across a wide parking lot off to the left. It looked like it used to hold something big, like a supermarket or one of those big-box stores. The building was flat, like everything else. I turned back toward the road... and stopped, whipping my head back to the left.

"Something moved," I said.

Hank continued driving. "What? A deer? Got a lot of those out —"

"It's a person," I said. I could see a man standing just off the parking lot in the scrub brush. He wasn't moving, but something about him was off. "Looks infected."

"No *way*," Hank said, slowing the jeep and following my gaze. "We cleared this place out."

"Couldn't one of them just walk in from somewhere else?" Rosa asked.

Janine turned to look as well. "It's possible, but we come through here a lot. We took everything the least bit valuable out of that supermarket before we knocked it down." Hank turned the jeep back toward the parking lot. I had my eyes trained on the spot where I'd seen the zombie. Another one appeared. A woman, from what I could tell.

"There're two now."

"Shit." Hank pulled into the lot, jumped out of the idling jeep. He grabbed a metal baseball bat jammed into a tube on the jeep that was probably originally meant for a fishing rod. "Where?" I pointed. Hank looked, saw the two zombies, began walking toward them. "Wait here," he said without turning back to us.

We watched Hank approach them. As the zombies noticed him, first the man, then the woman, they became enraged. They rushed at him side by side. His first swing probably destroyed the left patella and lower femur of the woman, young and pale, with a rat's nest of black hair. She gave an inhuman shriek and fell. Hank looked to finish her, but the other zombie — an older, pudgy bald man with dark skin that might have once been brown but was now a sort of gray — was already upon him. With an upward swing, Hank shattered the zombie's jaw into his skull, killing him instantly. He fell in a lump. Beside Hank, the female zombie gnashed and flailed, reaching for him, pushing toward him with her good leg. Hank took a second to plan his attack. Deliberately, he swung hard into the left side of her head, and we heard a combination crack and pop. Her dead body dropped beside the other zombie.

As we continued to stare, Hank inspected the scene, then turned to walk back to the jeep. He made it three steps. "Behind you!" he yelled, pointing.

Rosa and I turned and ducked in a fear-induced reaction, looking toward the cemetery on the other side of the road. Janine was better trained. As she pivoted in the direction that Hank was pointing, she pulled out her handgun, saw a tall, skinny infected man rushing at us from between the grave markers, and fired. The first shot grazed his shoulder, and he kept at us like nothing happened. Janine fired again, hitting him in the throat, and he fell in a gurgling rage of blood, flipping his body left and right on the ground next to a pockmarked gravestone. Hank climbed into the jeep, got it moving. When we looked back, we saw another zombie shambling in our direction.

Hank turned to Janine. "Radio it in. I don't know what the hell's going on around here, but we need to re-sweep McCormick." Janine picked up the CB.

After hearing what happened, Harvey made his decision. "You all keep going," he said, his voice as sure as ever, even through the crackle of the radio. "We need that equipment. I'll get some others out to McCormick to clean it up. Good luck."

* * *

We took 221 south along the eastern side of the lake until finally, at the southern tip, we turned right and crossed over the dam. It was still in one piece, although from the dead quiet I'd say its hydroelectric generators must have ground to a halt years ago. We continued south and west through the woods until finally we connected with Interstate 20. That took us almost due east, into the western fringes of Augusta. Marian had told us to look around the hospital there, because there were several labs in the area. We found the first of them behind the hospital, off Wheeler Road, in a collection of small, evenly separated brick buildings with neat, long parking lots — the standard configuration for medical buildings before the outbreak.

"Which one?" Hank asked Rosa.

"How the hell should I know?" She shrugged. "Let's try this one." She pointed to a small, ornate, tan building with a sign out front that identified it as a medical lab.

Hank pulled up in front, turning the jeep back toward the road for the fastest getaway in case it was needed and we got out. The plan was for Janine to stick with the jeep. We each had a walkie-talkie that had been charged at The Oasis. They only had six total, so the four they handed out for this mission was a testament to the importance of what we were doing. We checked all four of them to be sure they were in working order. I grabbed a tire iron from the jeep, and Hank got his bat. At his side, he also had a pistol. Rosa refused to carry any sort of weapon, saying she wouldn't know what to do with it anyway. Then the three of us headed toward the door. The day was bright, and we could see into the building through a panorama of large broken windows. While the place was a complete mess, it seemed to be empty. I thought it must have been ransacked dozens of times, especially in the first year or two of the outbreak, and began to wonder how many labs we'd have to hit to get the supplies we needed. Hank peered in the open windows, then went to the front door. He tried the handle, and the door swung open easily. He looked back at us, maybe trying to reassure us, maybe gauging our mettle. Probably both. He must have been satisfied with what he saw; he went inside, and we followed, Rosa in the middle and me bringing up the rear.

We passed through the destroyed atrium of the front lobby. A large corporate logo was half on the wall, half strewn across the floor in pieces. A desk of some dark wood sat topped with marble where a receptionist would have sat. Wires remained, but the computer that must have been on the desk was long gone. For a moment, although the space was larger and much more corporate, it reminded me of the waiting room at the office of my practice, and another lifetime of memories sprang up. Giving an amoxicillin prescription to a worried mother whose son was wheezing with a sinus infection, setting a broken tibia for a man who fell from the loading dock at his job, recommending an oncologist for an old woman who came to see me thinking she'd eaten something rotten. I realized I'd paused in the lobby as the others moved ahead, so I shook the cobwebs out of my head and continued after them.

Hank led the way through a door and down a hallway, but without the swagger he'd shown earlier. I could tell this wasn't his bread and butter. He was unsure of himself, looking for things he didn't really understand in a place he'd never seen before. As he moved away from the lobby, the light grew dim, so he turned on his flashlight. We each had one, plus a backpack to carry things out. Hank looked back at us. "In here?" he said, gesturing to a doorway.

"Try it," Rosa said, nodding. Hank prepared himself, pushed open the door, holding his pistol forward and swinging his light through the space in an arc. The room was narrow, with counters on each side and rows of shelves above them. A small sink beset with some sort of mold was embedded into the countertop on one side. The room had been gone over, who knows how many times. There were supplies strewn everywhere, hanging from shelves, on the floor, many torn open. After a quick check, Hank let Rosa enter the small room. She looked around quickly with her own small flashlight, grabbing a few items, mostly for sanitation, and stuffed them into her backpack. In a couple of minutes, she turned back to us. "That's all in here."

Hank radioed Janine to tell her all was well, then pushed forward down the hall, passing an open bathroom and an office with a debris-covered desk. He rounded a corner, leading us farther into the back of the office. The light from the front windows all but vanished. On the left, a door read STORAGE. Hank waited for us to join him, then opened the door with the same sweep of light as before. The room had been tossed, but remained full of supplies. "This looks promising," Rosa announced with a smile, pushing past Hank. "Come in here!" We all entered the room, and Rosa grabbed boxes, test tubes, a tabletop centrifuge, plastic bottles, and an assortment of sealed paper packages, jamming them into any backpack where they would fit. "Wow. We lucked out here," she said. "This stuff must look useless to most people.... Well, I guess it actually is useless for most people. But we're lucky to find all of it intact."

"Did you find everything you need?" Hank asked, hopefully.

"Yes and no." She swirled a plastic bottle in her hand, peering closely at it with her flashlight. "This agar powder is the biggest question mark. Conditions in here may have turned it bad. I want to get as much as we can before we leave. Can we look for more here?" Hank and I looked at each other and shrugged. *Why not?* We zipped up our bags full of everything Rosa had found.

Hank led the way again, into the hall, deep into the back of the building. On the left, he saw another closed door and moved toward it.

As he opened the door, we were immediately blinded by light. How was that possible, here in the back of this dark building? Hank swung his pistol and flashlight in an arc, but for a moment we were all blinded by the piercing glare. After a moment our eyes adjusted, and we could see we'd reached the far side of the building and were standing outside a room full of medical equipment. The light came from a door on the far side of the room that stood open onto the back parking lot. Machines glinted in the sunlight. Hank squinted and turned back to us with a wry smirk. "Guess we could've just come in that door," he said. Then we all heard a low rumbling.

Not a rumble. A *growl*. Hank jerked to attention, whipped the flashlight back through the room. In the back, under a space in the countertop probably meant for a chair... there were *eyes* looking back at us. First two large ones, then additional pairs, smaller, all catching the light. Hank pointed the pistol and flashlight directly at the eyes, and we saw... dogs. Or *a* dog. A momma dog, I presumed, and several pups. The pups looked at us in surprise and fear. But the mother bared her teeth in a vicious snarl. The growl grew louder as she realized how close we were to her litter. Hackles pleated her back as she took a step toward us. She looked to be a mutt, but a bulky, powerful one. Maybe part Rottweiler, perhaps part Bull Terrier. Her coat was a mix of black and brown. We stepped back, jamming the space with our bodies. I positioned myself between Rosa and Hank, putting her at the back of our ranks. If anything happened to Hank or me, it was important that Rosa get back alive. That the supplies get back, too. As we moved, the mother dog leapt forward a foot or so, asserting her authority. Could we blame her? Three strangers had just invaded her home.

Suddenly a shadow fell across the back doorway as another dog stepped into view. The daddy, I presumed. He was huge, much larger than the momma, skin bursting with muscles, and now he too began to growl, teeth bared. We stepped farther away. And they came for us.

I had my own gun, but only Hank had any kind of shot through the doorway. The female broke to our left, while the male went to our right, forcing Hank to decide which was the eminent threat. He chose the male. Not really aiming, he fired two or three times toward the rushing dog, hitting it more than once and ending its attack in a high-pitched yelp of pain. Whether dead or just injured, we didn't know. There was no time. We turned and ran, Rosa leading me, with Hank following behind. The female caught him at the turn of the hallway, grabbing his ankle with her teeth. Hank fell to the floor, his gun and flashlight clattering out in front of him. Rosa and I turned as Hank kicked at the dog with his free foot. She twisted and shook his leg in a rage, seemingly trying to tear it off his body. Hank screamed in pain.

Without thought, I raised my pistol and fired, hitting the female in the hindquarters in a broad splash of blood that sprayed the white walls. Another pained yelp. The dog released Hank, and he pushed himself up and lurched toward us. "Go, get out of here!" he yelled. We turned and ran, Hank limping beside us. He still had the sense to radio Janine. "Look alive, we need to move!" he said into the walkie-talkie. We passed back through the lobby and made for the front door. Through the shattered front windows, we could see Janine had backed the jeep up directly to the door and was waiting for us. We pushed outside, jumped into the waiting jeep, with Hank last of all. Rosa and I helped pull him into his seat as Janine gunned the engine. At that moment, the wounded, bloody mother dog ran out of the slowly closing front door and leapt at the side of the jeep beside my leg. Janine thrust into another gear and the jeep accelerated, leaving the dog behind. As we burst onto the main road and pointed toward home, Hank looked back toward the building, where the dog stood still barking at us. "I wish I had brought the damned grenades," he said.

* * *

Hank took off his boots and inspected his ankle. It was red and swollen, but there were no puncture wounds. Luckily, he had taken to wearing very thick construction boots, and while the pressure from the strong jaws was intense, I could see there would be no lasting damage. Janine guided us back the way we came as Rosa inspected the backpacks in the daylight.

It turned out that we brought back everything Rosa had on her list. But then she needed eggs.

20

After using the new equipment to make cultures, Rosa put samples of the flu into fertilized chicken eggs and incubated them. Then came the risk she had to make someone else take. Since Rosa had already been cured, she couldn't test the solution on herself. But in two days time, a family of three came into The Oasis, with their little girl already in the process of turning. She had been bitten by an attacking zombie while the family slept in a tent two nights before they arrived. It was amazing they all made it to The Oasis on foot after that. Rosa talked it over with Marian, and took the girl to the lab. They decided to try the egg solution. Cracking an egg, Rosa carefully went through a series of steps to extract the part she wanted into a beaker, then used pipettes to transfer the results into several test tubes. Loading those into the centrifuge we had recovered in Augusta, she set it spinning. After a time, she unloaded the tubes, extracted another portion using another pipette, and put that into a clean new test tube. She turned around with a tube half full of a milky, yellow-tinged fluid, looking at me with a nod.

"You're the doctor," she said, holding out the test tube and a syringe. Wordlessly, I prepped the needle and jabbed it into the girl's deltoid. In her feverish state, she put up no fight.

"A very small number of people are deathly allergic to eggs," I said while working. "If she is, she dies either way." No one seemed to appreciate my honesty.

But the little girl wasn't allergic, and she didn't die. In two days, she was alert. In five, she was out playing with the other kids.

Rosa had found a way to deliver a cure for the zombie outbreak, and it even came in a convenient carrying case, inside its own shell. She made dozens of egg cures. In just weeks, the original processing of new people was ended — no more saliva swabs, no more gurneys and restraints, no more anxiety and terror. Everyone who came in was just given an egg.

Soon, Rosa felt compelled to share the answer with the outside world. She talked to Harvey. "I want to take this to Atlanta," she declared.

Harvey, as usual, was nonplussed. "To the CDC, I assume?"

"Yes. I can show them how easy it is to reproduce, to transport. They can verify my results. We can tear down the city walls and go back to living." She was passionate about it, and Harvey agreed we should try.

"But it won't be easy," he said. "They aren't going to just swing open the gates for you."

I thought about nearly having been blown up on the highway. "Richmond shot at us," I said.

"Yep. Cities tend to do that." Harvey thought for a moment. "I can send scouts. We can test out the range of their guns and find a way to deliver your message without being shot on sight." As anxious as Rosa was, she knew it had to be done. Within an hour, Harvey had recruited Hank and Janine for the new job. The next morning they were on the way. We had to wait three days for their return. It wasn't good news.

21

Hank and Janine looked shaken. Harvey had gathered his inner circle, eight of the oldest and I assumed wisest citizens of The Oasis. Next to Harvey's office in the lodge, there was a large event room offering some privacy, so we met there.

"Atlanta fell," Hank said, with no preamble. "There's no one at the wall, and several pieces of it look like they've been torn down. There was a lot of smoke, too."

Janine took over. "A *lot* of people are streaming out of the city. They're looking for somewhere to go."

"Do you think they know where we are?" Harvey asked.

Hank and Janine shared a sideways glance, embarrassed, guilty. "Maybe," Hank said, looking down.

"Oh, my God, did you *lead* them here?" It was one of the inner circle, a thin, nebbishy older man with glasses, named Gerald. The rest of the inner circle looked around at each other; some made whispered comments.

"No!" Hank looked shocked.

"Hold on, hold on," said Harvey, raising his big hands. He looked at Hank and Janine. "What happened?"

Hank hung his head. Janine started, "He didn't do anything wrong."

Eyes locking on Hank, Harvey said, "Son, no one here is going to blame you for doing a job I sent you out to do. Just tell us what happened." Harvey glanced at the others, willing them to be patient.

"Janine and I have scouted around Atlanta many times before...," Hank began.

"The very reason I sent you this time," said Harvey.

"Right," Hank said. "So, we knew the area. We knew generally where the defenses were strongest. We took our jeep in on Interstate 20. It shoots directly into Atlanta going west, so we can get pretty close. They don't hold that area behind their wall, they're in the downtown and northern areas." He took a breath. "As we got near Grant Park, we knew we'd have to be on our toes. Around when there's the split for 75/85 North, you can see the downtown, all the tall buildings. There's a fence there, but it's too far outside for anyone to guard. It's good for cover, if you want to sneak up and take a look at downtown. We'd done it before, but we'd never seen anything like this. A few of the skyscrapers were on fire, the golden-domed one and some taller ones farther north. So we decided to come up to the southern wall as close as we could to see what was going on.

"Closer to downtown, Interstate 75/85 is the south wall. There isn't a lot of great cover around there, so we did it slow and stayed hidden. By the time we went a few blocks, we could *hear* them. There were people — lots of people — outside the wall." He paused.

"From there, we started to see people all over, but farther away," Janine said. "Lots of big groups, making caravans, headed somewhere. It looked pretty disorganized — people going everywhere. But a lot were headed east. We went in closer. I think we were just... *curious.* We'd seen the outside of their walls so many times, no one around, nothing but the possibility of getting shot. And now there were people."

Hank took over the story again. "So we were trying to sneak around... and we stumbled right into a group of people standing in the parking lot of a small old building, some kind of old store." Hank dropped his head again, but kept talking. "They were loading guns, gear, food, water — all into some pickup trucks. We tried to go by without them seeing, but..."

"But you don't *look* like them," Harvey offered.

"Yeah. The city must have just fallen within a couple of days. They were all still trying to be really clean, really neat. They had on those synthetic clothes everyone wears in the cities, so when they looked at us, they just knew. They could smell it on us and see it in every fiber of our clothing — that we were different." Hank set his jaw, drumming his fingers on the table. "A couple of them, they had another look: *infected.* But I don't think the people with them had noticed it yet. One of them was even the driver of one of the pickups."

Gerald interrupted. "You saw a *zombie driving a truck?*" There were gasps.

"We saw him behind the wheel," Hank said. "And he came after us along with the others. So, yeah." Hank looked around the table, at all of us, like he was willing us to understand how seriously he meant this.

Harvey thought it over. Then Anya, the oldest-looking woman in the circle, spoke up. "I guess we shouldn't be surprised. Rabid animals experience a period of behavioral change, they don't just immediately become hyper-reactive. With RL2013, the disease acts even more erratically. Sometimes the various stages are longer or shorter. An infected person might have many days when they can still maintain normal functions — including driving — even though they're progressing downward into dementia. But an infected person behind the wheel of a car..." She trailed off.

"Would be like a lunatic guiding a missile." Harvey completed her thought. We all stared at one another until finally Harvey turned back and asked Hank and Janine to finish their report.

Janine took a breath. "We dodged them all we could. We thought we'd lost them by the time we made our way back to our jeep. We took side streets to stay unnoticed; they must've taken the highway the whole way." Harvey nodded, silently prompting her to continue.

"When we finally got back on to 20 East to make time, we saw them in the rearview behind us. But not just those couple of pickups. There were dozens of vehicles. They weren't too close to us then, but we stood out. We were the only moving thing on the road in front of them. It was too easy to follow us."

Hank had been nervously drumming his fingers the whole time Janine spoke, but now he stopped. "As soon as we saw them, we knew we had to try to send them in some other direction," he said, "so we got off 20 and went south toward Macon." Hank pulled out a worn paper map to show us. "We did a bunch of zigzagging to try to throw them off. We saw them follow us south, a whole huge bunch of them. But we really don't know how far they went that way, or how convinced they were."

"Especially since there are rumors," Harvey mused.

"Yeah." Hank shuddered.

Harvey addressed Rosa and me. "We know from people coming into The Oasis that they've heard rumors, at least throughout Georgia and South Carolina: *Go to the border lakes.* So if these people from Atlanta have heard the rumors, we could be in for a whole lot of company."

Janine nodded grimly. "That's what we're worried about."

Rosa and I exchanged a careful, noncommittal look. This didn't seem like the time to let them know that some rumors had made it at least as far north as DC.

Vincent, another member of the circle, snapped. "We're doomed! I mean, we're *done* here, folks." He had the frantic, smiling sarcasm of someone who thinks there's nothing left. "Kiss The Oasis *goodbye!*"

Harvey's stern voice stopped Vincent. "How many?"

Hank returned Harvey's frank gaze, dead serious. "Based on the number of people we saw, if half of them make it out here, we'll be overrun."

Harvey stared at the scouts for a minute, thinking. I knew he'd been through a lot as the leader of The Oasis, but this was a challenge to dwarf all others. Then he spoke. "We can't support an entire city of people, and we can't turn them back if they want to come in. So now what?"

Harvey's eyes traveled around his inner circle. No words passed. Where before they'd blurted out what they thought or felt, now we witnessed the full effect of Harvey's strength. Through force of will, he kept them from losing the self-control, the sanity and judgment, he knew he needed from each of them. He looked to each one in turn. In my mind, I assumed he was saying, "What would you do? If you have an idea, speak it now." No one said a word.

After a long while, Harvey said, "We're peaceful people. Here's what we're going to do. We're going to set up a new perimeter, as far outside the current walls as we reasonably can. Every able person will help in the effort. There are lodges all through the lake areas, not just here where we are. We'll stop them and tell them that we can save them, as long as they'll do it our way. We'll cure them of the disease if they come to us peacefully."

It was a brilliant plan that had no hope of ever working.

22

The first of them arrived that night, in vehicles of all sizes: cars, trucks, RVs, tractor-trailers. Regardless of our planning, they would have broken through, and did. The time we had to make a new perimeter wall was not enough. To my knowledge, Harvey was never even able to present his offer of a cure in exchange for mutual peace. By the time our scouts raced to tell us outsiders were coming, it was too late. The new perimeter — a wide arc of thick wooden posts from freshly cut trees, not even half-finished — crumbled like tissue paper. Then the real gate did, too. There were groups of men with guns, families, women caravanning together, kids scattered among them all. Too many, too enraged. Not infected, just too worked up with fear, adrenaline, and desperation to think straight. They plowed through our defenses just to get at what we had: safety, serenity. They paid no attention to the fact that their destruction was the antithesis of what they had come for.

People died. Their people, fighting their way in. Our people, holding the gates, or protecting their loved ones at every lodge door and campsite. Once the main gate was breached, their vehicles streamed in. But it was a small road, narrow, bordered by Hickory Knob's dense woodland. They all tried to get in at once and quickly jammed up. Cars and trucks were locked against each other, with new arrivals piling up behind them by the dozens or the hundreds, or maybe even the thousands. From somewhere far outside the gate, past the new perimeter, we heard a terrible noise that sounded like the end of all things. At least for The Oasis, it was.

The awful noise grew, a gnawing, grinding din that soon absorbed all other sound, turning more and more heads, until finally everyone, all of us, people of The Oasis and the people from Atlanta, seemed to be stopped, staring, waiting. And finally, there it was. Emerging from the back of the line, clawing through it, crashing into cars, trucks, people, came a tractor-trailer dragging a huge tanker of gasoline. In a perfect world, or just a better one, this would have been a blessing — fuel for countless uses. Here, it was the worst of all possible scenarios. The huge truck drove through the smaller vehicles like a bowling ball through pins: everything was crushed, shoved aside, flattened.

Rosa, hearing the commotion, raced to the lab and grabbed as many eggs as she could in an effort to protect her work. Then she and I were dodging through the chaos, racing for some kind of safety. Without thought, we made for the only shelter we'd known since we left DC: the RV. But the roar of the incoming semi stopped us. As the truck approached, lights from the lodge buildings clearly illuminated the driver. His face was snarling, eyes wild. He made manic gestures, blood streaked across his cheek. He had the disease, and somewhere on the road from Atlanta, he must have turned. Now, our worst fear was smashing through the gates of The Oasis.

The truck slammed into one of the buildings on the north side of the lodge, flipped, exploded. The tanker of gas disappeared in a fireball beyond belief. Rosa and I were blown backward by the blast, blinded for a time. The entire building and anyone near it were torn to shreds, then burned on top of that. The zombie driving was incinerated. If only he'd known he was steps away from a cure, would that have done anything to change his actions? At that stage of the disease, I doubted it.

Through the smoke and flames, I saw Harvey standing in front of the ruined lodge, shouting orders, but I couldn't hear what he said. My ears rang. A group of young men confronted him, and he tried to block their path. One of them impaled him on a long, sharpened stick, and left him on the lawn to die, gurgling blood. Rosa shouted Harvey's name. We both sobbed. It was pointless. He was dying or already dead. Only escape would matter now.

Ironically, the same semi that destroyed the lodge had plowed an open path through the crowded road out, pushing aside all the vehicles that had been clogging the way. Rosa and I saw our only chance. We got into the RV and started moving. Confusion was our advantage; before anyone else could fill in the gaps, we shot toward the gate, now a ragged, gaping maw.

About halfway there, a handful of cars and trucks started to move again, swerving back toward the road, right into our path. Rosa rolled down her window and shouted, trying to make people turn their attention in different directions, away from us. Whatever it was that she yelled, it made people move. Again, Rosa's mind saved us.

With new vehicles continuing to pour in from the south, the road was rapidly becoming jammed again. We cut off into the woods, where the RV took a terrible beating. We drove slowly, both to preserve the vehicle and to avoid detection. Eventually, we met up with a state road running north. It was eerily quiet. We stopped for a moment and listened. Back in the direction of the camp, there were muted explosions, screams, sounds of pandemonium. Rosa reached for me and hugged me, tight, still crying.

From out of the woods on our right, a figure lurched, illuminated by the moonlight. A zombie, spasming and angry, stepped onto the road. He was maybe 25, strongly built, filthy hair that might once have been blond. He looked brutal enough to tear the door off the RV and rip us apart. Rosa gasped, gripping me even more tightly, but the zombie walked right past the front of the RV and didn't look at us. He was clearly drawn toward the light and noise from The Oasis. Then we looked down the road. There were two more zombies, then four, following in the broken footsteps of the first. With new urgency, I hit the gas and we started back north, leaving heaven on Earth dying behind us.

23

The next morning dawned, and we were still driving. We had turned east, then back north, once again traveling on the big highway, Interstate 95. It was mostly a random decision. I was in a daze behind the wheel. Rosa sat motionless in the passenger seat, the carton of eggs in her lap.

After a long time, she said, "We have to try to tell them in DC."

I was silent. In Richmond, they'd shot at us. In Atlanta and even Augusta, things just fell apart. Two people and a carton of eggs were now supposed to drive into DC and save the world? I scoffed. "What?" Rosa asked.

"I think it's impossible," I said. "We'll be tossed out. Or killed before we ever get in."

She turned in her seat. "Look at me." While driving, I spared a sideways glance. "I've never said it, but I love you. You mean almost everything to me. But the one trump card there is, is *this*." She gestured to the egg carton. "This is what I — no, what *everyone* has been looking for, for 10 years. If we don't do everything we can to get this to the people that can use it, we're less human than the zombies." She paused. "If *I* don't do everything I can to get this in the right hands, I won't be able to live another second of this life." She waited for my answer. Rosa was like that. She made passionate arguments, then sat back and let you digest them.

I thought about what she'd said. But I already knew my answer. I gave her another glance, looking into her eyes as long as I could. "Anything in my power to do to help you, I'll do. And I love you, too."

We had to stop to scavenge gas four times, but still made it to DC in under 12 hours.

24

If Richmond had enough defenses to nearly blow us to bits, we knew DC would be risky beyond belief. We approached the outskirts slowly. Unlike Richmond, DC had a big river guarding its southern flank. That helped us. As we drove up 395, we curved into view of the Potomac and of the classic Washington, DC, landmarks — the Washington Monument, the Capitol in the distance, the Pentagon right next to us. We stopped. I had no idea what to do next. Rosa led us off the highway. She said she wasn't quite ready. We found a small hotel and chose a room. It was a mess, but we could rest and think there.

Rosa told me she needed a few specific items, and the next morning we started looking. In a boating store in Alexandria, we found a flare gun, and in an abandoned police car, we found a bullhorn. The boating store had enough flares that Rosa took a few, assuming at least one would be good. But finding a battery for the bullhorn was another story. We spent more than an hour rummaging through convenience stores and gas stations to gather a handful of batteries, all of which had an expiration date years in the past. Back in our hotel room, she tried each battery until she found a combination that offered enough power to bring the bullhorn to life. "It only has to work once," she said, winking at me. Then she sat and gathered her thoughts. We both assumed this was a one-chance deal. Finally, we returned to the highway overlooking DC.

Rosa held the bullhorn and flare gun. I had the egg carton. We both hoped we were out of range of any cannon or gun the people on the wall might have, but knowing the government's penchant for military expansion, that seemed unlikely. We took the chance anyway, because there didn't seem to be any other options. And it seemed unlikely the guards would waste a lot of ammunition on two people who weren't even approaching.

Rosa looked at me. She smirked. It was the same smirk from so long ago, back at Eastern Market, on the other side of the river we now stood beside. I nodded. She raised the flare gun and fired. The fact that it worked startled even us. There was a blast, then a slow, fizzling, reddish ember burned and descended through the sky. Across the river, we could see people — just everyday people — who had noticed it. Thankfully, the world outside the cities was a relatively silent place these days. When Rosa lifted the bullhorn to her lips and spoke, I was pretty sure the people on the other side of the river heard her words.

"Government of Washington, DC, and the United States," she began. "We have come bearing no ill will whatsoever. In fact, we bear a cure for the disease. This is not a joke. My name is Rosalinda Menendez, and I worked for the NIH branch lab on Capitol Hill until I escaped the city a few months ago. I worked for the government every day for nearly 10 years to find a cure. What I found, outside the city walls, was that we were looking in the wrong direction. We were trying to eradicate all disease, to cleanse the body, when really we needed to realize that the body is part of a complex ecosystem and *must* have some infections, some bacteria, some viruses, to remain an effective organism.

"My companion and I traveled to South Carolina and found The Oasis. It really did exist, but it's been destroyed now that Atlanta has fallen. I'm sure you can verify that via your own methods. At The Oasis, they learned that patients who were infected with a strain of influenza — possibly avian — became cured of the zombie disease, even if they were in the process of turning. I spent some time researching this, and discovered that the particular strain of flu The Oasis used is a virus with bacteria add-ons that are vital to the overall cure. RL2013, the disease that has come so close to wiping out humanity, is part rabies and part leprosy. Rabies is a viral disease. Leprosy is a bacterial infection. The similar tandem of virus and bacteria in this flu strain seems to eliminate the virus and bacteria in RL2013. It even gives what seems to be permanent resistance to future infection."

She paused, looked at me, smiled. We couldn't see the faces of the people on the opposite shore, but I imagined them staring, some looking incredulous. A single spark can start a fire. Rosa was igniting new sparks with every word.

"We have here a carton of simple chicken eggs. Any of my former coworkers at NIH can tell you that eggs are effective for carrying vaccines. Each egg contains the flu strain needed to cure the zombie disease. From these few eggs, we can make hundreds, thousands, even millions of additional copies, to send around the globe and *end this disease for all time and for all people!*" Her words echoed across the Potomac, crashing into DC like waves of hope. In that millisecond, I could not have been more proud, more in love.

Her temple exploded before I even heard the shot. She fell. I didn't even think, just dove for her. The eggs flew out of their carton and broke onto the unforgiving gray pavement of the highway. Rosa, blind in one eye, looked up at me with the other, pleading. She couldn't speak.

I clutched her with force enough to drive the life back into her. Held her in my arms, my multi-colored bracelet touching hers, and willed her to live, with every word of conviction I knew. She was the savior of the world, come back to the city, the place that tried to take her away once before, come back to rescue them from their deepest fears. My tears ran with her blood. She died there, on that strip of roadway, in minutes. No idyllic resting place, just the hard tarmac of the street below her. I looked at the splattered eggs, the last hope for humanity. I thought, momentarily, about salvaging some of the fluid. Then a shot tore through my pants leg and ripped a chunk out of my calf. I turned my head toward the city. As I did, another shot missed my cheek by millimeters. I ducked.

In what seemed like hours, I looked at Rosa and said goodbye. I pulled away my hands and eased her down onto the roadway. Another shot. I rolled away, behind the RV. There was a general commotion in the city now, and it didn't seem to be coming from the wall defenses alone. After a beat, I ran and tumbled over the guardrail. I stumbled back to the side streets and found the hotel.

25

I'm back at the hotel room. I came here in a complete daze, no idea what to do. Now I know. There's no point in saving the world if it doesn't want to be saved — or at least if the people with the power don't want to give up that power so that others may live free. All I care about right now is Rosa. She doesn't deserve to spend her last moments as a human — alive or dead — sprawled on a highway, outside the city that killed her. Through my tears, I have decided to retrieve her body, and to take her somewhere else and bury her properly. Maybe The Oasis is calm again. Maybe she could go there? I don't care, I just can't leave her *there*.

These people. These *civilized* people. She told you what she had. And you killed her.

What have you done? Damn you.

I'm going to get her body now.

THE END

The story continues with

The Hopeless Pastures — The Oasis of Filth — Part 2

and concludes with

From Blood Reborn — The Oasis of Filth — Part 3

Thank you so much for reading my book! Here's a little bit about me, Keith Soares. I live in Alexandria, Virginia, with my wife and two daughters. By day, my wife and I run a web, mobile and app development studio, which means that writing is my second job. Creativity has always been a huge focus for me, whether making music, coding video games, drawing or writing. *The Oasis of Filth* is my first published novel.

Visit my website at **http://keithsoares.com** for information on other books and upcoming projects. While you're there, I hope you consider joining my mailing list where I can keep you updated on future books.